THE REBOUND Play

KATE O'KEEFFE

Map of the Town

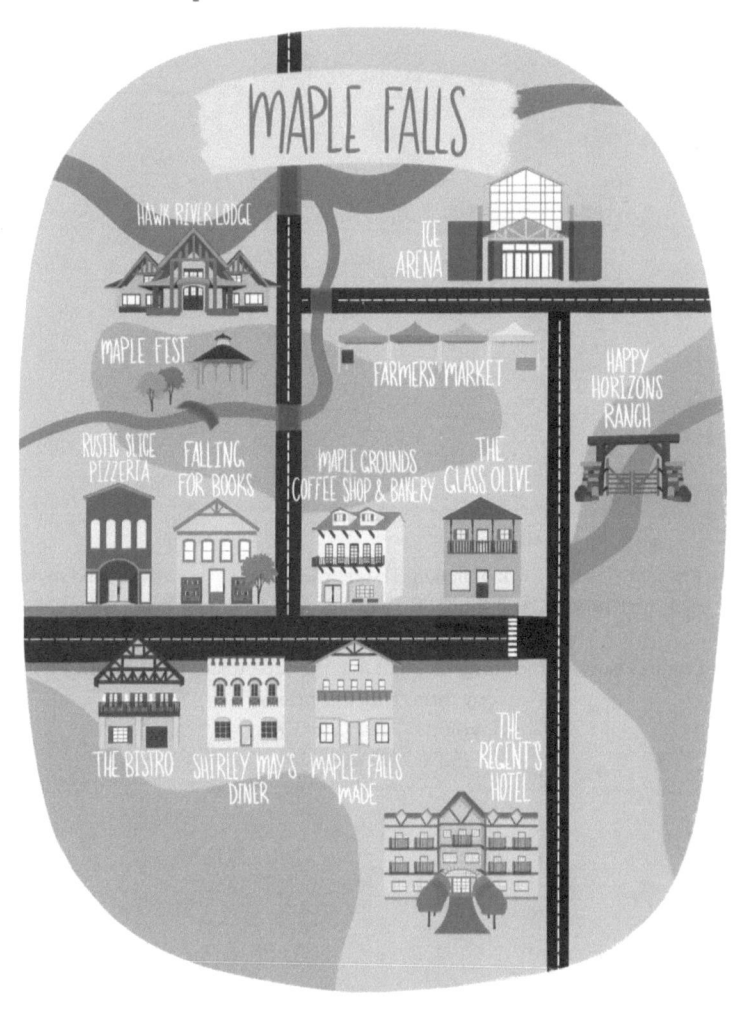

The Rebound Play is a work of fiction. The characters and events portrayed in this book are fictitious. Any similarity to real persons, living or dead, is purely coincidental and not intended by the author.
All rights reserved, including the right to reproduce, distribute, or transmit in any form or by any means.
Copyright © 2024 Kate O'Keeffe
ISBN: 9798329933260

Wild Lime Books

CHAPTER 1
DAN

I REACH for the remote to silence the game on TV as I listen to my former teammate and mentor, Troy Hart, on the other end of the line. I've been lounging on my oversized sofa as I recover from my latest PT session. Being benched for a left wrist injury during the Chicago Blizzard preseason wasn't exactly the way I planned things to go this year, and I'm frustrated I'm not fit to be out on the ice with the team.

But Coach's word is law in my world, and he's benched me for the next five or six weeks.

I'm about as happy about it as a polar bear in a sauna.

I put the phone on speaker and sit upright. "Wait. Did I hear you right, Troy? You want me to come back to Maple Falls to play hockey for a kids' charity team called the Ice Breakers?"

"That's what I said," he replies.

"But there is no kids' charity hockey team in Maple Falls."

"There is now, thanks to me and Zach, my loaded brother. He's matching the sponsors' donations, and all proceeds from the games will go to charity."

Zach Hart, billionaire. *Huh.* The idea of that fancy guy in my small hometown in Washington state is almost laughable.

"Which charity?" I ask.

"Happy Horizons Ranch. Angel Davis runs it. She's a local here in Maple Falls."

"Angel Davis? I've known her just about since birth."

Troy laughs. "Maple Falls sure is a small town. Angel does a great job helping disadvantaged kids learn outdoorsy skills on her ranch. Kids come from all over the county these days."

A worthy cause for sure.

"You know I'm down with an injury, right?" I ask, instinctively rotating my left wrist to assess the pain.

Yup, there it is.

I hurt it at practice last week, smashing into the plexiglass in an uncompromisingly aggressive hit from the team rookie. It turns out plexiglass is a lot tougher than my wrist. I told Coach he was overreacting when he benched me, that it was just a sprain. But he wasn't listening. Said I was too important to the team to compromise. Said he's got his eye on me as captain once our current captain, Carter, retires.

I should take it as a compliment. All I am is frustrated.

Time on the ice back in my hometown sounds more than tempting—once my wrist is healed.

"I do know you're injured. I also know you desperately want to play, and you're benched with the Blizzard."

"Do you know everything?" I joke.

"Yup," is his straightforward answer. "I can give you ice time as captain of the Ice Breakers, right here in your hometown. Perfect, right? Game time *and* family time."

I always went on about how great my hometown in Washington state was when Troy was on the team, and clearly, the guy was listening. He and his wife, Kelly, bought an arena when they moved there not that long ago.

As he is older than me and was already a gold medal Olympian and top NHL player by the time I joined the team straight out of college, I've always looked up to Troy. He was the elder statesman of the team. If Troy says come home and play hockey for a kids' charity, I'm not going to question the guy—particularly when he's offering to clear it with my team management.

"Keep talking," I tell him as I lean back against my seat, the cream leather groaning against my bulk. What can I say? We hockey players aren't exactly known for our small frames. I'm 6'5" with a decent amount of muscle and shoulders my high school coach once described as wide enough to block out the sun. I'm no ninety-pound weakling, and if I were, I wouldn't be able to do what I do for a living.

"It's a six week commitment, including practice time and five games against the Canadian Lumberjacks. And it'll be great for your state of mind. Being benched for an injury is no picnic."

"You got that right," I grind out.

Troy laughs. "I remember the days when not playing a game felt like the end of the world. But trust me, Dan, there is life outside of hockey."

"You sure about that?"

"Positive."

"I want to be out there, playing my part. This season we've got as good a shot as any team of winning the Cup."

I'm not being arrogant. I know I'm a good player. I got drafted in the first round, right out of college, and I've got a seventy-six-point average per season. Not bad for a small-town boy whose hockey-obsessed dad had to take a second job at the gas station to afford my sport.

Now, being able to pay off my parents' mortgage, as well as take them on a cruise of their choice each summer, is my way of paying back their sacrifice, despite the fact they're always telling me their pride in my success is more than enough.

I know I totally won the family lottery, from my actor brother, Ethan, right down to our book-obsessed kid sister, Emerson, aka Emmy. Mimi, our grandmother, lived just down the street, always feeding us delicious baked goods from her kitchen, and instructing us not to tell our mom. We're close, supportive of one another, with a set of parents who might not have had much when we were growing up, but who went beyond the necessities for each one of us. For me it was hockey lessons and running me around for games, for Ethan it was acting class, and for Emmy it was an endless supply of books.

"I get it. Hockey's your world right now," Troy replies. "Which is why coming back to your hometown to play is so perfect for you. I can work things out with your team management to get you the time off, and we've got an excellent PT. She'll get that wrist back into shape before you know it."

"I've got to admit—it's tempting."

And besides, there's another reason for going back home, and it's kind of a big one. Keira Johnson. My Kiki. Only she hasn't been my Kiki for ten years now.

Just the thought of my high school girl—the girl I left behind—has my pulse kicking up a notch or ten.

Keira is the girl I've never been able to forget.

Sure, there've been other girls. It's been a long time and I'm no saint. Women tend to throw themselves at you when you're an NHL player, particularly when you're known as the pretty boy of the team. Those puck bunnies, as they're sometimes called, simply come with the territory—and it's fun territory, believe me.

Of course, the fact that my kid brother is the current heart-throb on the hit Netflix fantasy show, *It Came One Winter*, doesn't exactly hurt, either.

But here's the thing: Most of the women I meet are only interested in me because I'm Dan Roberts, center for the Chicago Blizzard, brother to the guy they love to watch on TV. Relationships for me tend to last a few weeks, a month, tops. My lifestyle means it's hard to hold down a relationship. And besides, those women aren't interested in plain Dan Roberts, the hockey-obsessed kid from Maple Falls, who worked his butt off to make it to the NHL.

So, my heart has been safe, never forgetting my first love. Keira.

An image of her springs into my mind. She's laughing at something, her gray-blue eyes dancing, her blonde hair falling in soft waves around her shoulders. Her smile is framed with those cute dimples of hers, the dimples I used to get to brush soft kisses against.

I took her for granted when I had her. I was a dumb kid, only seventeen when we broke up. I figured there'd be other girls, other loves. It's been ten years since we broke up for me to take my hockey scholarship at Yale, literally the other side of the country from her. But I know if I ever got the chance to be with her again, trust me when I say I would leap at it.

"When do you need me?" I ask, my mind made up.

"Seriously? Dan, that's awesome! Having the great 'Dan the Man' Roberts, hometown hero and famous NHL star, on the team would mean even better media coverage and more money for the kids."

I laugh. "And I get to have some of my mom's home-cooked meals."

"On that, it would be good if you could stay with the team. Me and Kelly bought the Maple Falls arena as well as the lodge. You might remember it. The Hawk River Lodge?"

"The one on the edge of town with the big pool. Yeah, I remember it."

"I don't have to tell you it's nothing too fancy."

"There's nothing much fancy about Maple Falls," I say on a laugh. "But that's part of its charm."

"You're so right. Can you get here by the end of the month?"

My entire schedule consists of physical therapy and gym workouts. Occasionally, I catch up with the guys from the team, but it's hard when I'm not training with them, getting ready for the season.

Truth be told, I spend more time alone than I'd care to admit. I guess I've been so busy chasing success I've not created the life I actually want. But I tell myself that will come in time. Right now, it's all about hockey. I've worked too hard for it not to be.

There will be time for a wife, kids, a place that feels like a real home. As slick and spacious as my house is, it's never felt like a real home to me. Not like where I grew up.

Don't get me wrong: my life isn't exactly horrible. I've worked hard to get where I am, and I'm reaping the rewards, from the huge paycheck to the fame, and everything that brings.

As ungrateful as it sounds, it's not enough for me.

I want that special someone, someone to have a family with, someone to grow old with, someone who loves me for me and not the fame or the money.

And a big part of me has always wondered if that person is Keira. She still lives in our hometown. That much I know.

Spending a full six weeks in Maple Falls might just give me the answer.

CHAPTER 2
KEIRA

THE MARKET IS a riot of early fall colors. The lush greens and bright hues of summer are fading, replaced with oranges and rusts and reds, not only in the changing leaves on the surrounding trees, but in the produce in the market stalls: gourds and pumpkins and butternuts everywhere.

It's my favorite time of year here in Maple Falls, so named for the maple trees planted here by the town's founders, that well over 200 years later still reach majestically toward the sky. Their foliage provides shelter from the hot sun and rain clouds in the summer, and a veritable tapestry of rust and red and orange now in the fall.

I chew on my lip as I eye the empty stall, nestled between the Maple Falls Meats and Callie's Cupcakes. Where once Willy Watson sold his caramel walnut fudge now stands an empty counter, surrounded by the same cream canvas of all the Maple Falls Farmers' Market stalls.

It's only been empty for a week, but that's seven days too long in my books. I know. I've been running the Maple Falls Farmers' Market for the past four or so years, and the rent on these stalls is vital to its overall success. Busy stalls equal greater cashflow, and I need the market to make a healthy profit. I love this job and the last thing I want to do is let down my employer, Geoffrey Goldblatt and his son, Martin. I'm really hoping the Maple Fest gives the coffers of both the Farmers' Market and the city the boost we need.

"You're looking pretty serious there, Ms. Keira Johnson," Brian says, pulling my attention from the empty stall. Brian's the proprietor of Maple Falls Meats. He has a store on Maple Road and a stall here at the farmers' market each weekend. He's a hardworking, burly, friendly guy, commonly found wearing a white apron over his round, plaid flannel-clad belly.

I smile. "I'm working out who we're gonna put in this stall now that Willy's retired."

Willy Watson was a farmers' market fixture, kind of a Maple Falls local legend. It was he and his wife, Nancy, who first suggested expanding the Maple Falls Farmers' Market from simply selling fresh produce, flowers, and plants to include items from local businesses, such as baked goods, coffee, and ice cream. The waffle stand is particularly popular, and I can't say I'm adverse to the treat, smothered in cream and strawberries, at the end of a long day. Willy brought in local bands that lend a relaxed and fun atmosphere to the market, and people can be found wandering around each weekend morning, clutching their coffees and hot chocolates, munching on bacon sandwiches and pastries, folk music filling the air.

Did I mention I love my job? Where else can you work in such idyllic surrounds?

After graduating college in Seattle and coming back to Maple Falls, I worked at the coffeehouse in the bookstore my friend Emmy runs, until this job came up. Although I was tempted to do what my college friends were doing—moving to big cities to pursue exciting careers—I knew I needed to be back home. My sister, Clara, and I lost our parents in a car wreck when I was a freshman at college. And then, disaster struck again when she got so sick with chronic fatigue syndrome, aka CFS, that she could barely get out of bed, and her scum of a husband left her and her two young kids for another woman.

She needed family. I was all she had.

Of course I wanted to try out a different life, at least for a while. But it wasn't in the cards. So here I am, twenty-seven years old, living in my hometown, with no plans to ever leave.

Don't get me wrong: I love living back here. The place has got heart, just like a small town, only with some of the amenities of a much bigger place. I mean, what small town has an ice arena? Other than Maple Falls, that is.

It's so picturesque here, and many a tourist can be spotted at this time of year, lapping up the local scenery and snapping shots of the pretty leaves. And attending the Maple Falls Farmers' Market if I've done my job right.

"Those sure are some big shoes to fill, Keira," Brian comments, bringing my wandering mind back to the market. "Willy was an integral part of the fabric of this place."

I pull my lips into a line, feeling the pressure. "I've had a few applications, so I'm trying to work out what fits best between Callie's and your stalls."

Let's face it, raw meat and freshly baked cupcakes aren't exactly a match made in heaven. The applications I've received so far have been from a butcher from a neighboring town, which as I make a cup of tea. Spotting the kids out the window, I see that Hannah is already in her figure skating outfit, and when I wave at them, they rush back into the house with excited squeals, almost bowling me over with their enthusiasm.

"I'm the captain and you're my prisoner!" Benny exclaims.

"You're not going to make me walk the plank again, are you?" I ask.

"The plank! The plank!" he chants in response.

"Let me get my swimsuit first," I tell him as I tickle him under his arm, and he falls down giggling.

I notice a tear in Hannah's tights. "Honey, how did this happen?"

"It got caught on a twig," she replies, placing her hand over the tear. "It's not my fault."

"Do you have another pair you could go change into?"

She shakes her head mournfully, and I make a mental note to buy her a new pair next time I'm in town.

"We don't have time to sew it up now, but I'll fix it tonight and get it back to you before your next lesson, okay?"

"Thanks, Aunt Kiki," she replies dutifully, although I'm sure she doesn't want to wear patched up tights when some kids in her class have brand new everything.

We've got to make do with what we can afford. With Clara not being able to work and her idiot of a husband not only out of the picture, but only providing erratic child support and alimony, it's up to me to hold this family together—and more than just by making tea and hand-sewing up tears in tights.

Supporting my sister and her two kids might not be the way I saw my life turning out, but you do what you've got to do for the people you love.

"I'm going to deliver this drink to your mom, and then we're ready to go. Go get your warm clothes. Layers are our friends on the ice," I tell her. That and cinnamon rolls. I stuff three into a paper bag to take with us to the arena.

Hannah dashes from the kitchen in a blur of excitement,

THE REBOUND PLAY

trailed by Pirate Benny, still ha-haring as he goes. Hannah loves her figure skating class, and I'm so lucky my friend and ice-skating teacher extraordinaire, Ellie Butler, gives us a hefty discount on both the classes and her skates. Figure skating is an expensive sport, and with Benny chomping at the bit to try ice hockey, I'll take whatever discounts my fellow townsfolk are willing to offer.

You only get one childhood, and I want to make theirs the absolute best it can be.

A few minutes later, I've delivered Clara's tea, made her more comfortable on the sofa, grabbed my current read from my nightstand, and the three of us have headed to the arena. Once there, Hannah runs in through the door in excitement, her blonde ponytail flying, and we follow after her, Benny far less enthusiastic to have to watch his sister's class.

A brisk chill wraps around us, a stark contrast to the relative fall warmth outside. The air carries the distinct scent of ice, mixed with a hint of hot chocolate drifting from a nearby stand. I can hear Ellie's encouraging tones, mixed with the crisp scrape of blades on ice as she stands in the middle of the rink, her breath fogging the air as she teaches a class of older kids.

She notices me and throws me a quick smile, and I wave back.

"Did Hannah help you with your homework?" I ask Benny, holding his hand in mine as we make our way to the bleachers. Hannah is a typical older sister: like a little mom-in-training who loves to boss her brother around.

"I hate math. It's so hard," he complains.

"What's hard about it?"

"Everything. It hurts my brain."

"I know what. I'll help you with it. I'm not the best at math, but I know enough." And how hard can first grade math be? I'm banking on *not hard at all*.

"Can I go to Levi's house to play when we get home instead? He's a pirate, too."

"Of course you can, but how about we give this math thing a shot first? I promise it'll be fun, and you might even be surprised with how much you already have in that big brain of yours."

He pulls his lips to one side, not convinced. "I guess."

I help Hannah lace up her skates as she chats eagerly with her classmates, ready for her class. I kiss her on the head and tell her to have a good lesson before I find Benny and me a spot alongside the group I've labelled the Mom Squad in my head.

"Hey, everyone," I say as I sit, the cold metal of the bench instantly beginning to seep through my clothing. I pull out a coloring book and crayons from my purse and hand it to Benny, who begins to color.

"Hey, Keira," says one of the moms, a woman called Nell. She was a few years ahead of me at Maple Falls High and is now married with a couple of kids. She glances at the book in my hand. "Watcha reading this time?"

"*Wuthering Heights*. I read it back in high school, so it's a reread for me," I reply. "It's good, despite its doomed love story between the two main protagonists, Cathy and Heathcliff."

"Yeah. Sure." It's clear Nell has zero interest in my book. "Have you heard the big news?" she asks, her eyes bright with excitement.

I put my bookmark in my book and close it. "What news?"

"Well, you know how Troy and his billionaire brother are hosting those charity games coming up soon?"

Of course I've heard about it. It's the biggest thing to happen to Maple Falls in … well, forever. Zach Hart has come to town and invested in Troy's hockey team, which means a bunch of top hockey players will be here to play a bunch of charity games to raise money for the Happy Horizons Ranch. It's a worthy cause, and I plan to attend all the games, like the rest of the town.

"I live here," I reply with a light-hearted roll of my eyes. "What's the latest?"

"Dan Roberts is back here right this very minute, ready to play on the team. *The* Dan Roberts, as in hometown hockey hero and NHL superstar? My friend who works reception at the Hawk River Lodge told me. Can you believe it?" Nell's expression shows me just how thoroughly excited she is by this news.

Me? My heart seems to have stopped at the mere mention of his name.

So, the rumors were right. He's back in town.

Dan Roberts.

My ex.

I had called Ellie a couple days ago in a panic when I first heard he may be on the team. She'd teased me about him, suggesting we could rekindle things while he's here.

But, you see, the thing is, Dan Roberts might be our hometown hockey hero, he might be big news in the NHL, but to me, he's always been my *what if?* The one that got away.

Only he didn't get away, exactly. I let him go. Back in the day, we were high school sweethearts in the flush of first love when he won a hockey scholarship to Yale. I was going to college at the University of Washington, so I would be at the other end of the country from him. Everyone told us a long-distance relationship would never work, particularly because we were so young.

There'll be other guys.

There are plenty more fish in the sea.

So, even though it broke me, I told him to go. We broke up.

I told myself at the time I had big plans of my own. I might not have been on a sports scholarship at a top school, but I knew I wanted to make something of myself. When everyone tells you at seventeen your high school sweetheart is only your first love and not your last, you believe them. And besides, I didn't want to be the one to stand between Dan and his dreams. Breaking up was the right thing to do.

Or so I thought.

It turns out they were wrong.

Dan was my first love, and although it's only been ten years since he left Maple Falls, no one else has even come close.

Breaking up with him was the hardest thing I've ever done and my heart has never recovered.

And now he's a big star, big goal scorer for the Chicago Blizzard. He's talented. Famous. Women love him. He leads this crazy, glamorous, exciting life. A life I know nothing about.

Me? Not famous. I glance down at my jeans, sneakers, and red puffer jacket. Definitely not glamorous. What's more, I'm still living in the small town I grew up in. I'm just plain old Keira Johnson—never changed, and probably never will.

Dan's a big hockey star, coming home to play on the Ice Breakers team, and I'm just his high school girl.

I haven't seen him since we broke up. Not officially, anyway. As embarrassed as I am to admit it, I saw him last winter. He was at the diner downtown, enjoying a meal with his family, home for the Christmas holiday. I was in a booth in the back with Hannah and Benny, and as soon as I laid eyes on him, I slid down in my seat so he couldn't see me, making it a game for the delighted kids. Then as he was posing for selfies with fans, I bundled the kids up and snuck out the back as quickly as I could, much to the surprise of the kitchen staff.

Mature, right?

But when the guy you've never been able to forget turns up in town, looking irresistibly handsome and thoroughly happy with his life's choices, you do what you've got to do and, in this case, that involved me pretending with Hannah and Benny that we were spies and needed to ninja roll and then crawl—quite literally—out the back door. Shirley May, our regular server and a kindly resident of the town, unlocked the door for us, and we climbed into my car, and slunk away without even switching on the headlights.

The kids thought it was super fun. I thought it was super *necessary*.

I knew seeing him could stir up a whole load of feelings that would be far from helpful. And seeing him so happy? Well, I needed to protect my heart. Pure and simple.

And now, today, I know it makes sense that people are excited about him coming back home to play on the charity team. Dan's the local guy who went off to play in the big leagues. He's our hometown hero, Maple Falls' answer to Sidney Crosby. He's big news around here.

The fact he's also the ex I've never been able to forget? Well, that's really only big news for me.

CHAPTER 3
DAN

I ADMIT it's weird to be back in my hometown for a full six weeks, rather than for just a handful of days. Of course, I've been back since I left: holidays, birthdays, stolen long weekends when I could fit them in. My parents, Emmy, and my grandma Mimi, all still live here, and sometimes it's nice to have a place to retreat to when I need to get away from the NHL and everything that goes with it.

But in all those visits, I've not met up with Keira, not even once in all the years since I left. I've not even bumped into her accidentally. Maple Falls isn't a big place, so it's weird, almost as though she's been actively avoiding me.

But that makes me sound paranoid. I guess the truth of the matter is, our paths simply haven't crossed.

If I have my way, all of that is about to change.

I park on the leafy street outside my parents' house, the home I grew up in. The big tree in the front lawn still has a swing hanging off it, and the white picket fence, although freshly painted, is the one I used to jump over after school each day.

Sometimes it pays to be tall.

The front door swings open and out strides my dad, trailed by my mom. Their faces are beaming, happy to see their oldest son home.

I climb out of my rented SUV and bound over to them, jumping right over the white picket fence, just like I used to. I collect both my parents in a bear hug.

"Mom, Dad."

"It's good to have you back here, son," Dad says as he slaps me on the back.

"Let me take a look at you." Mom holds me at arm's length, looking me over. "How's your wrist, honey?"

"It's getting better."

"I wish you'd have let us get you from the airport," Mom scolds.

"I had to pick up my rental anyway. I saved you the trip," I explain.

"Do you have time to stay a while? I know you're busy," Mom says.

"Your mom made her famous pumpkin pie," Dad adds.

As if I need convincing.

"Is that my grandson?"

I turn to see Mimi standing in the doorway, her silver-gray hair tied up in a neat bun at the nape of her neck where her habitual string of pearls rest, her face crinkled into a wide grin.

"Your favorite grandson is home, Mimi," I say as I place a kiss on her forehead, breathing in her familiar floral scent.

"I don't see Ethan," she replies with a wink, naming my brother.

"You always were the comedian of the family, Mimi," I reply with a smile. "Is Emmy here, too?"

"Your sister is too busy running that bookstore," Mimi pronounces. "She works too hard, and then she spends the rest of her time looking after me."

I wrap my arm around her waist, and together we walk into the house. "It's only because she loves you. How's your arthritis?"

She waves my concern away. "Oh, you know how it is, sweetie. Any day I'm upright is a good day."

"How about that pie, honey?" Mom asks when we reach the kitchen.

My mouth waters at the thought of one of Mom's home-cooked pies. "Sounds good to me." I look around the kitchen, at the old linoleum floor, the tired cabinets, and the old-fashioned oven. "The place hasn't changed. You know I'm happy to buy you a new kitchen."

"Spend your money on yourself, son," Dad says, his chin held proud. "You've done more than enough."

"Your father is right. You've done a lot for us," Mom agrees.

I open my mouth to protest, but we've been down this road before. I've offered to replace their kitchen many times, but the answer is always a firm but polite "no." It's a miracle they allowed me to pay off their mortgage for them. It's a small win, but I'm taking it.

"Now, we've not told your sister you're in town yet because we thought it'd be nice for you to drop by the bookstore and surprise her," Mom says as she slices up her pie.

"I'll drop by tomorrow."

"Oh, Emmy will be thrilled," Mimi says.

We sit around my parents' kitchen table, catching up on each other's news over Mom's delicious pumpkin pie until it's time for me to go.

"Your old bedroom is waiting for you if you want it, honey," Mom says as I ready myself to leave.

"I know, Mom, and I promise I'll come back and visit whenever I can. But Troy wants the team together to bond quickly, since we're only playing five games total. We all play on different teams, so there will likely be some rivalries. It kinda goes with the ice hockey territory. I know this isn't the big leagues, and all the money we make is going to charity, but you know me. I want to win our games. We're more likely to do that if we know how the others tick—at least on the ice."

"We're so proud of you coming home to play to raise money for the Happy Horizons Ranch," Mimi says. "It's such a worthy cause, teaching disadvantaged kids farm skills and the like."

Dad asks, "Will you be able to play with your wrist injury?"

"That's the plan, Dad. I've got a month to fit in as much physical therapy here as I can before the first game. My PT back in Chicago seems to think it's doable, and Coach gave me the go ahead to come here to play for the Ice Breakers, so if all goes well, I'll be fine for the first match."

"You're the captain of the team. You need to be fit and ready to lead," Dad says.

"Yeah." I know there's a lot riding on me being fit and able. I just hope I recover fast enough.

"Don't we have such wonderful children?" Mom says with a smile, her eyes glistening. "We're lucky to still have Emmy here in Maple Falls, though we don't see enough of you and your brother."

"I watched Ethan on that show of his," Mimi declares, and we all look at her in surprise.

"But Mom, it's a violent fantasy show. I wouldn't have thought it was exactly your cup of tea," Dad says.

"But Ethan is my cup of tea. I watched it on the Netflix," she replies proudly.

My grandma watches *It Came One Winter* on Netflix? And she calls it "*the* Netflix?"

"How, Mimi?" I ask.

"Emmy showed me how to watch it on television. I'm hooked," Mimi says, her eyes bright.

"It is a good show," Dad agrees, shooting me a look.

I wrap my arm around her shoulders and give her a squeeze. "Good for you, Mimi."

Soon, I tell them I need to get going, and promise to catch up with them all again soon. I wave goodbye and head to the Hawk River Lodge, the place Troy and his wife Kelly own, and where they're putting up the guys on the team.

Like my family home, it hasn't changed.

When I push through the glass door to the lodge's reception, there's a brunette at the front desk, who begins to flick her hair and adjust her top when she spots me.

I don't recognize her, but it's clear she has some preconceived ideas about me. In my line of work, I get that a lot.

Glancing at her name tag, I smile as I place my suitcase on the tiled floor beside my feet. "Morning, Denise. I've got a booking for—"

"Dan Roberts," she finishes for me, her eyes bright. "I know who you are. *Everyone* knows who you are. You're 'Dan the Man.' Dan Roberts. Chicago Blizzard center. Maple Falls born and bred."

"Thanks," I reply as she gives me my life story. I never know how to respond when people say things like that. And anyway, what exactly am I thanking her for?

Thanks for knowing who I am?

It's great that I'm famous enough for you to recognize me?

Nope.

"It's so good to have you here as part of the Ice Breakers, Mr. Roberts."

"Dan, please."

"Dan," she repeats, letting out a giggle. "Everyone is so excited that you're here. You're one of the first player to arrive, in fact, *Dan Roberts*," Denise continues, weirdly using my full name.

"I like to be early. Get the lay of the land before all the excitement starts."

"Get the lay of the land? You grew up here, Dan Roberts!" she points out.

Why does she keep doing that?

"True, but I've never stayed here at the resort. And you can call me just plain Dan, you know. It's only one syllable. Nice and short."

She winks at me, her face starting to shine. "Sure thing! No one told me you'd be funny, too."

When she continues to grin at me, her face warm enough to fry eggs, I ask, "Do you need me to sign something to get the room key or something?"

"Key. Right," she exclaims as though just now working out that I might need one of those to access my room. "Coming right up." She rummages around behind the desk until she produces an actual key, attached to a large wooden key chain in the shape of a maple leaf.

"Wow. An actual key. You don't get those a lot these days," I say as I inspect it. It's surprisingly heavy.

"We're old school here. Old*ee* world*ee* charm and all that." She pauses before she adds, "*Dan*."

"Sure. Well, thanks, Denise. You've been real helpful." I turn to leave.

"Don't you want to know where your room is? I gave you the best one at the lodge. The billionaire guy isn't staying here."

She must mean Troy's brother, Zach Hart, the billionaire involved in financing this whole thing. I've met him a few times. He's a good guy, and not what you'd expect a self-made billionaire to be.

"I appreciate that. Where is it?"

She tells me the room number and says, "You're right next to Dawson Hayes. Do you know him?"

"Sure do. We played on the same team back in college."

It'll be great to see my old college teammate. He played for the Carolina Crushers last season, but I heard he's moving to a Seattle team next. It'll be like old times, out there on the ice with the guy.

"Nice. Your room overlooks the river. I could take you there, if you like? Everyone here knows you've got an injury."

"They do?"

"Of course they do. Your team coach mentioned it and now everyone knows. You're our hometown hero. We pay attention to that kind of news."

I give her a self-effacing smile.

"Let me carry your suitcase." She stands bolt upright, her chair crashing to the floor behind her in her haste.

I raise a hand. "No, it's fine. You're needed here, I'm sure, and I've got two hands."

She beams at me as though I've said something incredible. "You bet."

"Has Dawson checked in yet?"

"Not yet. Most of the players are booked in from tomorrow. I can check, if you want?"

"No need. Thanks."

She grins. "Sure. Will you be heading to the arena after? Check it out again after all this time?"

"Absolutely. A lot of great memories at that rink."

"I know. My mom told me."

Her *mom*? How old does that make me? I've only just turned twenty-eight.

I throw her a smile before I turn to leave. "That's … err … great. Thanks."

"Have a great rest of your day, *Dan*."

After locating my room, I drop my bags, grab my hockey bag,

and head to the arena. I haven't caught up with Troy in quite some time, and I'm eager to see him—and the rink where apparently Denise's mom remembers me playing.

I really admire Troy and I've always viewed him as a mentor. He's very generous with his time and his resources. I'll never forget how kind he was to me when I was starting out as a rookie. He's a good guy. One of the best.

When I enter the arena, there's a kids' figure skating lesson going on, taught by a pretty brunette I recognize from my high school days, Ellie. I catch her eye and wave at her, and she grins back at me.

I glance around until I locate the offices. Figuring Troy will be there, I make my way around the rink. As I approach a group of people, who I assume are the figure skating kids' moms, there's an audible titter among the group, and every eye seems to land on me.

"Hey, there," I say with a smile, to more tittering.

"Dan Roberts, as I live and breathe," says one of them, a woman with dark blonde hair, probably in her early thirties. She's holding her hand over her chest, her face beaming. "Would you look at you."

Which is exactly what she does, her eyes roving over my hoodie and tracksuit.

"Well, aren't you the hometown hero come back home to roost," she declares.

I've got no idea what that even means.

"We are so pleased you're here, Dan," another woman says, this one older, with salt and pepper hair and thick-rimmed glasses.

"Mrs. Nelson?" I ask.

"You remember me," she says with a smile.

"How could I forget you? You taught me all I know about Shakespeare, which isn't a whole lot, I'll admit," I say to my old high school English teacher. "Do you have a kid skating right now?"

"A granddaughter. That's my Violet in the fuchsia." She points at the group of kids, and I spot a short, dark-haired girl in pink, concentrating hard on her teacher's instruction. Beside her is a girl with a tear in her tights, performing a pretty dang-perfect-looking turn.

Not to be outdone, the woman with dark blonde hair says, "My daughter's the one with the bright yellow headband. Dani's her name. She loves figure skating, and we all love hockey, especially you, Dan."

There's a murmured agreement among the ladies.

"That's so kind of you to say, and I'm so happy to be back here, playing for such an important charity," I reply, and they all titter some more, agreeing with me.

There's a sudden thud and a woman screeches at the back of the group, half laughing, half in shock. "What are you doing?!"

A few heads turn, and I think I spot a couple of sneaker-clad feet, under the seats.

"Why are you lying down? You're silly!" a young boy says with a laugh.

"Is someone hurt?" I ask, dropping my bag and bounding up the steps two at a time.

There's an audible "Shhh!" before someone mutters something I can't quite hear.

"Keira? Are you okay?" says a woman with curly red hair, sitting directly in front of the sneaker-clad feet as she turns to see what's going on.

Wait. Keira?

"I'm fine," comes a muffled but stern and familiar voice.

Is that …? Could it be …?

Keira's here? My Keira? Well, not my Keira anymore, but you get what I mean.

With my pulse quickening in my temples, I climb the final step to see a figure lying flat on her back beside the bleacher, a hood obscuring most of her face, some sort of baked good that looks a lot like a cinnamon roll clutched in her hands. But what I

THE REBOUND PLAY

can see of her mouth, the cut of her jaw, the blonde hair falling down her shoulders, I know it's Keira.

What I can't work out is, what the heck she's doing, lying down on the cold, hard floor between two benches of the bleachers, surrounded by a group of chortling moms, here at the arena on a Saturday afternoon.

CHAPTER 4
KEIRA

WHAT AM I *DOING*?!

   I mean, sure, I got the fright of my life when I looked up from my book, mid-bite of my cinnamon roll, to see Dan Roberts standing in front of me, chatting with the moms as though he doesn't have a care in the world. Because of course he doesn't have a care in the world. He's a famous and wealthy NHL star. He's got it made. And he's looking shockingly good, with his dark hair kind of messed up but sexy, his tan skin glowing as though he just stepped off the beach. His jacket is open, revealing a white T-shirt that more than hints at the muscular torso beneath. He looks effortlessly hot in that unattainable, famous person way, like he's from another planet, simply visiting us mere mortals here on Earth.

So, what did I do? I panicked. *Big time.*

I knew it was only seconds before he would look up and clock me. I also knew that I had successfully managed to dodge the guy every time he visited town for the past ten years, and I needed to keep that record for my sanity.

So, I did what every self-respecting, twenty-seven-year-old woman would do: I dropped to the floor and pretended like I wasn't there, clutching my half-eaten cinnamon roll to my chest as though it was Harry Potter's invisibility cloak.

Sadly for me, it's just a cinnamon roll.

I know, I know! Not my best move. But needs must, people! I had to get out of there without him seeing me, and with no exit in sight for me to slink out of undetected, I did what I had to do.

The fact that not only did it not work—thank you, Nell—but now I can feel the eyes of the one person I wanted to hide from boring into me like lasers, just adds to my utter humiliation.

Gingerly, I lift the hood that's covering my eyes a fraction, only to see Dan towering over me as he takes in this prostrate woman, bizarrely lying on the hard floor, heating it up with her own mortification.

Nell must realize that she messed up because she says, "She's fine, Dan. I think she just dropped a contact."

A contact. Yes! I'm looking for my contact. That's a totally plausible explanation for why I am where I am.

"But she's lying down, flat on her back," I hear Caroline say. "She doesn't seem to be looking for anything. Just ... resting. Which is beyond weird. Keira? Are you sure you're okay? You're not having a fit or something, are you?"

"She's not epileptic."

"People can become epileptic, you know. It happened to my cousin's friend when she was about fourteen."

Note to self: sit farther away from Caroline and the rest of the moms next time I bump into an ex I've been hiding from for ten years.

Not that I hope *ever* to repeat this particular scenario.

Dan clears his throat. "Can I help look for your contact, miss?"

He called me miss? Phew! He doesn't know who I am.

"No, thank you," I reply, purposely making my voice a little lower so he doesn't catch on to who I am. "I've got it covered, sir."

Benny giggles before he squats down beside me and pokes me in the ribs.

So not helpful.

"Are you sure? Because from where I'm standing, you look more like you're simply lying down than looking for anything," Dan replies, and I'm certain I catch a note of amusement in his voice.

"Yup. Totally sure. Bye now," I say, waving my hand.

Benny giggles and pokes my ribs some more.

After a beat, I lift my hood a fraction only to see Dan is still standing there, only now he's reaching for my open book on the bleacher and picking it up.

Why doesn't he leave? Can he just chalk this experience up to some crazy woman who thought it best to search for her dropped contact by lying on her back?

But no. He's still here, and now he's got my book.

Wonderful.

"I always felt bad for Edgar in this book. He had a rough ride," he says.

If Dan knows it's me lying here, he'll know that I'm itching to offer my opinion. It's Heathcliff who had a rough ride in *Wuthering Heights*, not so much Edgar, even though, of course, the fact that Cathy married him without really loving him wasn't exactly great for him. But I'm not about to admit that to Dan right now.

It takes all my strength not to respond.

"Here. Let me help you up," he says, offering me an outstretched hand. "Kiki," he adds, and my face goes from burning hot to positively nuclear.

I know the game's up. I've been caught by my ex, trying—and failing—to hide from him.

I let out a defeated sigh before I bend my knees and take his hand, allowing him to pull me to my feet, my hood slipping off to reveal my true identity.

"Thanks," I say breezily, as though this kind of thing happens every day. "Oh, Dan. I didn't realize it was you."

We both know it's a bald-faced lie, but he has the good grace not to call me out on it.

"I didn't know it was you, either," he replies with a quirk of his lips. "Although the book was a bit of a giveaway. You always loved *Wuthering Heights*."

"It could have been anyone. A lot of people like that book, you know."

"Sure," he replies, those lips of his pulling into a fully blown smile.

Of course he thinks this is funny. He's just found me trying to hide from him like I'm a four-year-old at the playground, making the assumption that if I can't see anyone then they can't see me, either.

By now the blood in my veins has been replaced with liquid humiliation.

"That looks tasty," he says, gesturing at my hand.

I look down at the half-eaten cinnamon roll. "It's from Maple Grounds. You know, the bakery on Maple Road?"

"I remember it," he says softly, his eyes so intense, I swear they can read my thoughts. "It's good to see you, Kiki."

"It's ... good to see you, too." I do my best to pull my lips into a brief smile, my heart beating like a frenetic drum.

I just know the eyes of every member of the Mom Squad are

sliding between the two of us, hanging on every word we say. They'll be wondering why I tried my best to hide from Dan, probably putting two and two together. Some of them might even remember that we dated back in high school.

"You two dated, right?" Caroline says, as though reading my mind. "Back in the day? I was only a few years ahead of you both at high school, but we all knew about it. The bookworm and the jock."

"That's right!" Brooke, one of the other Mom Squad members says. "I'd forgotten about that. This must be some kind of reunion of sorts for you two, right?"

"I guess it is," Dan replies with a smile. "We've not seen each other since—" his eyes alight on mine. "When was it?"

"Let me think." I scratch my chin as though I'm searching my mind. But of course, I know exactly when it was. It's etched in my mind along with Dan's dimples, the touch of his skin, the feel of his lips on mine.

I clear my throat. "It was the end of summer after our senior year."

The memories of that last summer are seared into my soul. The time we spent up at the lake with a gang of friends, all of us on the precipice of adulthood, our future lives unfolding before us in a stretch that felt like it would last forever.

And then we broke up. It was the night before Dan was due to leave for Yale. We'd talked about breaking up. Neither of us wanted to do it, but we knew it was for the best. We said we would always be each other's first love, and at the time, that felt good enough.

But the following morning, standing outside the Roberts' family home, watching Dan's dad back down the driveway with Dan in the passenger seat, his eyes trained on mine, I had wanted to make the car stop. To tell him not to go, that we could work it out and do the long-distance thing.

That I could never imagine loving anyone else the way I loved him.

THE REBOUND PLAY

But I didn't do anything. I simply stood there beside his mom and his brother and sister, waving and smiling as though this was all part of life's great plan, and that I would move on to bigger and better things, always with a soft spot for my high school sweetheart.

Yeah. What did I know? Not a lot, as it turns out.

There was no other love. Dan was it. Period.

And I let him go.

"Dan the Man. It's so good you're back home where you belong," Caroline says and I shoot her a look, knowing she's stirring the pot.

She smirks at me.

Benny's eyes grow to twice their normal size when he takes Dan in. "You're him? You play for the Chicago Blizzard! You're the best!"

Dan smiles at him. "Sure am. And who are you?"

"I'm Benny," he replies as he takes a hold of my hand, gazing up at this 6'5" giant.

It's as though I can see Dan's thoughts flit across his face as I watch him. He's trying to work out where Benny fits into my life. Is he my son? My nephew? Am I babysitting? Why am I here watching a figure skating class with the Mom Squad?

His eyes flick to my left hand and I just know he's searching for a ring.

So, he thinks I'm married with kids. Part of me wants to put him straight, tell him that Benny and his sister out on the ice are both Clara's kids. Another part of me—the less rational part that thinks it's a good idea to hide on the floor of the arena—wants to pretend they're mine, that I did move on from him and have married the great love of my life, producing two beautiful children with him.

But this is Maple Falls, a small town fueled by two things: the lumber mill and gossip. I might not be the one to tell him I'm not a happily married mom of two, but someone else will before too long.

"Hi there, Benny," Dan says, bending down closer to Benny's height, which is a long way down for a super tall guy like Dan. "It's great to meet you."

"Did you know you're called 'Dan the Man'?" Benny asks with his gap-toothed grin.

"I did, yes," he replies.

"My mom says you're a hometown hero."

His eyes flick to mine. "Does she now?"

Ha! That less rational part of my brain does a little dance.

"Does that mean you're like Spiderman?" Benny asks, and some of the Mom Squad laugh at his adorableness.

"I think Spiderman is way cooler than me," Dan replies.

Benny shakes his head. "Nah-ah. Spiderman would be dumb on skates."

Dan chuckles. "I think you're right, but between you and me, I'm not sure my web slinging apparatus is quite up to scratch."

His eyes grow to the size of dinner plates. "You have web slinging appa-batus? You're so cool!" He looks up at me, his eyes shining bright. "Dan the Man is a superhero?"

"Of course he's not, honey. He's just messing with you," I say, feeling weirdly touched by the effort Dan is making with the kid he currently thinks is mine.

He shrugs. "It's true. I'm just a regular guy. Tell me, Benny, do you skate?"

He shakes his head. "I want to be a famous hockey player, just like you. But I'm not allowed." He looks up at me with a mournful look on his face—the one he gives me anytime ice hockey is mentioned—as though I'm the one standing in the way of his NHL hockey career.

"How old are you?" Dan asks.

"I'm six and two halves," he replies.

"Six and one half, Benny and the Jets," I correct gently.

"Six and a half is old enough to start learning how to play hockey. You could put him in a Learn to Skate program," Dan suggests, not helping at all.

But then how could he know that we can't afford for Benny to learn how to play?

"See? I told you," Benny complains to me, and I purse my lips.

Finally, Dan reads the proverbial room. "Did I say something wrong?" he asks me. "I did, didn't I?"

I shake my head. "It's fine. Benny's here to watch his sister's lesson."

Dan's brows pop up to meet his hairline—which I notice is exactly where it was when we dated back in high school. Nothing receding there. Still thick, luscious dark hair that a girl itches to run her fingers through.

Not that I'm going to do that.

"His sister?" he asks.

"Hannah. She's having a lesson with Ellie, right now," I reply, gesturing at the ice.

"All our kids are in that lesson. That's why we're here," Caroline says. "We love figure skating, but not as much as we love hockey. I'm Caroline. It's great to see you again. You probably don't remember me because I was a few years ahead of you in high school."

"Hey, Caroline," he replies, and then all the members of the Mom Squad introduce themselves, describing their tenuous connection to him as though sketching an elaborate family tree.

"Which one is Hannah?" he asks once he's humored them all.

"She's the one in the white hat and jacket," I explain, pointing at her on at the ice. If he sees the rip in her tights, he doesn't mention it.

"I noticed her when I came in. She's a natural on the ice. Talented."

I can't help but smile proudly as I watch her fluid movements. Next to some of the other kids in the class, who clunk around, looking stiff and uncomfortable, Hannah looks like she was born to skate.

I flick my gaze to Dan's and notice him watching me.

"Thanks," I murmur, heat claiming my cheeks.

"Dan Roberts!" a deep voice says, thankfully pulling his attention from me.

I look over to see Troy, the owner of the arena and the Hawk River Lodge, heading our way. He's accompanied by another big guy, who I can only assume is another member of the Ice Breakers charity team. Together, they're one imposing group, three huge guys in great shape with shoulders wide enough to form a bridge.

"Good to see you, Troy," Dan says as they shake hands warmly.

Troy slaps Dan on the back, his face lit up in a genuine smile. "I am so excited you're here. This is going to be an incredible six weeks. Right, ladies?"

They all enthusiastically agree as they gaze appreciatively at the cluster of men.

That's one positive aspect to this whole Ice Breakers thing: serious eye candy for the ladies over the coming weeks. I'm sure none of the women of the town will complain about that.

"Dan, I want you to meet Scotty MacFarland. He's the second coach for the team, working with Doug Strickland," Troy says, and I take the opportunity to slink away, leading Benny further up the bleachers as Dan and Scotty MacFarland shake hands in greeting.

Hiding behind my book, I watch the three of them as they discuss Dan's injury—something literally *everyone* in Maple Falls has been concerned about since he came out second best in a collision with the plexiglass during practice—my humiliation finally beginning to subside.

The first meeting with Dan is done. It might not have been as I pictured it, but then weirdly, I didn't picture myself lying on the ground, hoping to melt into the floor during our first meeting since we broke up. But at least it's over, and now I know that when I do inevitably see him again, it can't be nearly as awkward. We can meet as two impartial acquaintances, important to one another in the past, but no longer.

At least that's what I'm telling myself. That way it's so much safer for my heart.

CHAPTER 5
DAN

MY STUPID HEART has been doing weird things at the sight of Keira. Weird things that I know I can't entertain, not if she's married with kids.

Married with kids.

The thought hits me in the solar plexus like a train heading at high speed into a wall.

Could it be true?

I need to look at the evidence. Be level-headed about this. She's here with two kids, one of whom held her hand and blamed her for not allowing him to take hockey classes. Benny's six and a half and his sister looks to be about eight, nine tops. Keira would have had to have gotten married and had those kids pretty dang fast after I left town, but it's possible. Then there's the fact the boy—Benny—shares Keira's blonde hair and gray-blue eyes, the eyes I remember so clearly, gazing into, feeling as though my heart would burst with love for this girl on the precipice of womanhood.

The girl I had wanted to be with forever.

But surely, I would have heard about it if she'd gotten married and had kids? Someone would have told me. Mom, Dad, Emmy? But then I never raised Keira with any of them, which maybe they took as a sign that I didn't want to know about her. Maybe in doing so, they thought I was protecting myself?

And you know what? They would have been right.

But why wouldn't the news about Keira having kids have gotten back to me? It's not like the townsfolk around here don't love to gossip, least of all Mary-Ellen McClusky, the town gossip since I was a kid. I saw her on a trip to the market to pick up some groceries for my parents last time I was in town. She hadn't even mentioned Keira, much less Keira's marital status.

Despite not having heard a word, everything points to yes. I admit, I scanned her left hand for a ring and didn't find one. Maybe she doesn't like to wear a ring? Maybe it's in the shop, getting repaired? And besides, a couple of living, breathing, small humans trump a ring, anyway.

A lump forms in my throat.

Of all the scenarios I thought could play out when I saw my high school girl for the first time since we broke up, not once did it occur to me that she might be in love with someone else. That she might have fallen in love and be married with kids. That she'd well and truly moved on from me.

What was I thinking? Of course she's moved on. It's been ten years! Of all people, I know what a truly amazing person Keira Johnson is. Of course she's been snapped up by some guy, some guy I'm having seriously negative feelings about, right about now.

All this time I've been comparing every woman I meet with her and seeing them come up short, and she's moved on, gotten married, and become a mom.

I'm an idiot. A total idiot.

As Scotty outlines some of his ideas for training, due to start up in a couple days, I steal a glance at her. She's still as beautiful as she was back in high school—only more so. Not that I thought that was possible. Back then, she was easily the most beautiful girl in town. Her face has matured: her once plump face now less so, showing her high cheekbones. Her eyes are still the same gray-blue, her lips still full and luscious. Her blonde hair is cut shorter than it was when she was seventeen, falling softly just below her shoulders, framing her face.

She's the kind of woman you can't help but notice, but who you know isn't looking for attention.

We were opposites back in high school, her and me. I was the jock, always at practice, always with my teammates, playing games, hanging out. She was more of a loner, with just a few close friends, but a whole lot more studious than me. Some people called her a nerd back then, but they didn't know her. Not the real her. Sure, she liked books, and she did great at school, but there is so much more to her than just being bookish and smart. She always saw the best in people. She was kind, even to the people who labelled her, who questioning why a popular jock like me would go for a girl like her. Why not a cheerleader type?

I knew why.

Because they weren't Keira.

"Roberts? You with me?"

I pull my attention back to the two guys I'm standing with.

"Yeah. Just lost in some memories, I guess," I tell them.

Scotty glances at Keira. She's got her nose buried in her book

THE REBOUND PLAY

again and doesn't look up. "An old girlfriend or something?" he asks.

How the heck did he guess *that*?

Who am I kidding? I must have it written all over my dang face.

She's the one I could never forget.

I clear my throat. "It was a long time ago."

Scotty smirks. "She's pretty. Bookish, by the looks, but then you know what they say: opposites attract."

"She's smart. Smarter than me, anyways," I reply.

Scotty grins. "I always say when it comes to exes, it's best not to be an archaeologist."

I regard him quizzically. "Meaning?"

"Don't dig up the past." He grins at me as though his total dad joke was somehow funny.

"Archaeologist. Dig. I get it," I reply. It might not be funny, but this guy is one of my coaches for the next six weeks. I always find with coaches that it pays to get on their good side.

"You played for the Peaks, right?" I ask, purposefully moving the focus away from me and Keira.

Not that there *is* a me and Keira anymore. Or ever will be, by the looks of things.

I try not to let that idea take hold. I mean, I don't know *for sure* she's a mom or even married.

There's still hope.

"Yeah, it's been a while. I'm a coach these days, but I still like to get out there on the ice." He regards the rink with a look that can only be described as wistful, and I get the feeling he misses the game.

"It must be weird to come back to your hometown to play. I bet it brings back some memories," Troy says. "My wife Kelly and I are relatively new to the area. Did you play at this rink a lot?"

Memories of me playing in high school wash over me, of the

wins and losses, the highs and lows, of Keira always in the stands, cheering me on. Wearing my jersey.

Why are all roads leading back to her?

"Only every practice and half the games. I practically grew up on this ice," I reply.

"I bet you did," Troy says. "It'll be amazing for the townspeople to see you out on that ice again. I got some PT lined up for your wrist, as promised."

"Thanks."

"Yeah, I heard about that. How is it?" Scotty asks.

"It's improving," I reply.

"Do you think you'll be good for the first game in about a month?" Scotty asks.

"I sure plan to be. That's why I'm here," I reply. "Hey, thanks for smoothing things over with the team," I say to Troy. He had spoken with the Blizzard's management, getting them to agree to release me to play the charity games for the Ice Breakers.

"My pleasure. We're just glad we could make it happen. These games mean a lot to the town, and to the kids at the Happy Horizons Ranch."

I nod. "It's an honor to be here, captaining the team for the cause."

Movement in my peripheral vision grabs my attention. I look over to see Benny holding a hockey stick that's almost twice the length of him, pushing an imaginary puck around the floor. He's concentrating hard, as though he were on the ice, playing on a team.

I smile as an idea begins to form in my mind. He seems like a good kid, and he wants to learn how to play hockey. Sure, he's only six and a half, but that's not too young to start. Maybe I could give the kid a lesson or two? I glance over at Keira once more and to my surprise, I catch her watching me. Quickly, she averts her gaze, pulls up her hood, and immediately concentrates back on her book.

She may have moved on, but I could at least do something nice for her kid.

Yeah, that's what I'll do. I'll make Benny's day and offer to give him a few lessons. And, if by some wild chance Keira is no longer married to the father of her kids? Well, hope springs eternal. Not for her husband, of course—but for me.

"Cooper Montgomery is due here any minute," Troy says, pulling my attention back to the guys. "He wanted to get the feel for the place before the first practice. Or at least, that's what his publicist told me. Do you want to join? Just don't go compromising that wrist."

I gesture at my bag with my skates, pads, and sticks. Anything to get my mind from Keira. "Ready and willing," I say with a smile. "I've played against Cooper a few times in the past. He's a good player. But tell me one thing, does the guy ever smile?"

Both Scotty and Troy laugh.

"He's not known for his easy charm, but he's a solid right wing. He'll give you a run for your money on the ice, that's for sure," Scotty says. He focuses on something over my shoulder. "Speak of the devil. Cooper! Over here!"

A big guy who bears more than a passing resemblance to Travis Kelce trudges toward us, a thunderous dark cloud sparking above his head.

Cooper Montgomery.

"Cooper!" Troy exclaims, as he pumps his hand. "It's great to be working with you."

"It's good to be here," he replies, his positive words in stark contrast with the scowl on his face.

"Hey," I say, giving him a fist bump. "It's great to have you on the team. It'll make a nice difference from beating you in the League."

It's a facetious comment, and I flash him a grin as I say it.

But Cooper simply continues to scowl at me. "Yeah, something like that," he replies.

"Did you bring your gear?" Scotty asks him.

Wordlessly, he pulls his bag from over one of his shoulders.

"How about you guys head into the locker room and I'll meet you on the ice," Scotty says.

"You're gonna skate with us, Coach?" I ask.

"You know me. Frustrated player," he replies with a laugh.

"Come with me, guys. I'll show you to the locker room," Troy says as he turns on his heel.

I shoot Keira one final look before I turn to walk away. She's still got her head buried in her book, her hood up, pulling off an Obi-Wan impersonation.

When she looks up again, my chest is instantly filled with exhilaration. But she's not looking at me. She's watching her daughter's lesson.

Her daughter.

That exhilaration wooshes right out of me.

As I walk away, I can't help the words from ringing in my brain. *I missed my chance with the only woman I've loved.*

CHAPTER 6
KEIRA

WALKING into the Falling for Books bookshop is like stepping into another world. It smells like two of my favorite things: books and coffee. The shelves are stacked with all kinds of books, from literary fiction to thrillers to romance. There's a low hum of people chatting, and the sound of pages being flipped. This place is filled with a bunch of stories waiting to be read. An escape from reality.

And right now, escaping my reality is more than a little appealing.

Why does Dan have to look even better than I remember? He

looks better than the pictures I see of him online. Better than when I watch him play for the Chicago Blizzard on TV; and oh my, does he look good when he plays on TV.

And the way he looked at me at the arena? His eyes were soft, his lips quirking into an easy smile, showcasing that old confident Dan Roberts charm I knew so well. I may have seen countless images of him over the years, but they're nothing in comparison with the real thing.

The memory of how I hid from him squeezes my belly.

I think everyone could agree that it wasn't my best move, dropping to the floor and pretending I wasn't there. But everyone could see me, including the last person I would ever want to catch me doing something quite so asinine.

But if my seeing Dan has tilted my world on its axis, forcing me to dive for cover—literally—for him, it seems as though I'm just another acquaintance. Someone from his past who holds little relevance in his world today. He was so relaxed, so confident, like seeing me was no big deal at all for him.

I get it. It shouldn't be a big deal. We broke up a lifetime ago. He's moved on. He's got his big career and probably a super confident and gorgeous girlfriend who doesn't do dumb things like try to hide behind the bleachers, clasping onto her cinnamon roll.

I blow out a breath in a vain attempt to calm myself. But abasement like that burns hot, and I know my cheeks are as red as my sweater.

The first time I saw Dan I had planned on looking totally poised and ridiculously hot in some gorgeous dress and heels combo, my hair and makeup just so, so that his tongue would hit the ground as I sashayed past him, saying, "Good to see you again, Dan. We must catch up some time," or some other such breezy, I'm-over-you words.

Clearly, that was not meant to be.

It's going to be impossible not to see him again. Troy's brother, Zach Hart, the big billionaire who's helping to finance the Ice Breakers, has given free tickets to the first game to every family in town, and I know Benny would never speak to me again if I didn't bring him along to each and every game.

I bite down on my lip.

Who am I kidding? It's never going to be easy to see Dan, knowing that he's moved on. I'll just have to be strong. Show him I'm fine with everything. He has his life and I have mine.

But just as I've come to this conclusion, I envision him and a couple of the other guys on the team as they made their way onto the ice following Hannah's lesson. Wearing Ice Breakers practice jerseys and holding hockey sticks and helmets in their gloved hands, my traitorous heart gave a squeeze.

Great start, Keira.

I spot my college friend, Blair Radcliffe, who I've come to meet for coffee at the cute café at the back of the bookshop and wave at her. She waves back, a big grin on her pretty face.

"How's Heathcliff working out for you this time?" my friend and bookshop manager, Emmy, asks as I walk past the counter, clutching my copy of *Wuthering Heights*.

Oh, and Emmy is Dan's sister, too. As the saying goes, you can run but you can't hide, especially in a small town like Maple Falls. That's for sure.

An image of Dan holding this very book in his hands flashes before my eyes and I must have a weird look on my face because Emmy adds hurriedly, "I get it. He's super brooding and intense. Even I can admit that, and I love the guy. I've got plenty of recommendations for you if you're not into the brooding type."

"It's not Heathcliff. He's great. I've just got a lot on my mind right now."

Like your brother.

Emmy's eyebrows raise. "Everything okay, Kiki?"

"Nothing I can't handle," I reply with a breezy smile. Or at least I hope it's breezy because I don't feel the least bit breezy right now. In fact, I may look like I've just eaten a bad burrito.

Emmy was a couple years behind me in high school, and

although we're friends, she has no clue how I still feel about her brother after all this time. Why? Because I should be over it. Any normal, sane person would have moved on a long time ago.

"Have you ... err, seen your brother?" I ask as casually as I can manage.

I can't help myself. Sue me.

"Dan? Not yet. Why? Is he here in town already?"

"That's what I heard," I lie because I really don't want to go into the whole "stop, drop, and die" incident with Dan's sister. "I'm here to meet my friend from school, so I'd better go. Great seeing you, though."

"See you at the first game?"

"Absolutely. Wouldn't miss it."

I make my way to the back of the store where I greet Blair with a warm hug. "Girl, it's so good to see you," I tell her as we sink into the sofa. "I can't believe you're here in my hometown for six whole weeks."

"It's all worked out so great: I'm here, all expenses paid, and I get to hang with my college bestie," she replies with a grin.

"I saw your guy at the arena. He looks super serious."

"Honey, the guy puts the grump in grumpy," she replies with a shake of her head. "But I'm representing him, so I gotta take the good with the grump."

"Lucky you."

"It's not so bad. At least he's yummy to look at. Hey, I ordered you a coffee. I hope you're still rocking the mocha?"

"Definitely. I can do with all the caffeine and sugar I can get right now, believe me."

She pulls her brows together. "Let me guess. A certain ex, who also happens to be an NHL star, is back in town?"

My gaze shoots to Emmy who, thankfully, is busy serving another customer and not listening in on our conversation.

"That's his sister over there," I say in a hushed tone.

"Seriously? This *is* a small town."

I shake my head at her. "We give Stars Hollow a run for its money, I tell you."

Being my college roommate, Blair knows all about the Dan and Keira show—and how I never got over him. She was my long-suffering bestie, there for me when I needed a shoulder to cry on whenever Dan's name would come up. And come up it did. Repeatedly. I learned that kind of went with the territory when your ex is some kind of hockey superstar.

When he got drafted to the NHL, our entire town held a party, right here on Maple Road in downtown Maple Falls. All the shops shut for the afternoon, and we had long tables covered in red and white check tablecloths heaped with food, and featuring commentary by every proud man in town grilling burgers and bragging about what part they had to play in Dan's success.

It was the biggest thing to happen to our town *ever*, and everywhere I looked, people were wearing Dan's Chicago Blizzard jersey, talking about him, and showing their pride in his achievements.

Don't get me wrong. I'm proud of him, too. But it's way more complicated for me.

The barista, Neesha, the daughter of one of the farmers' market stall owners, delivers our coffee, and I introduce Blair before she returns to the counter.

"Do you know everyone in this place?" Blair asks.

I shrug. "Sure."

"Whoa. That is trippy." She leans back on the sofa, cradling her coffee in her hands. "Okay. Spill the tea. Have you seen your ex?"

I begin to blush furiously. "Oh, yeah. On Saturday. I kinda embarrassed myself at the ice-skating rink in front of him."

"Seriously? What happened?" She takes a sip of her coffee. "Not bad."

"It's either coffee here or at the bakery. There's not a lot of choice on the coffee front in this town. Not like in Seattle. We were totally spoiled for choice there, remember, B?"

"No deflecting. Tell me your embarrassing story."

"Do I have to?"

"Yup."

"I saw him and made a snap decision to ... hide," I tell her reluctantly.

"As in rush to the ladies'?"

I press my lips together and slowly shake my head. "I dropped to the ground in the bleachers. I thought I could hide."

As I utter the words, I can barely believe I did it myself.

"You did *what*?" She tries to keep the grin from forming on her lips.

"I lay down behind the seats, hoping he wouldn't see me."

"And did he?"

I twist my mouth. "He kinda helped me up."

"Oh." Her nose is scrunched up in secondary embarrassment for me, and I can tell she's holding back a laugh.

"You can laugh. I know you want to."

Her shoulders shake as she does just that.

"Got it out of your system now?"

Blair pulls her features into a concerned look. "I'm sorry you felt you had to do that."

"It was the worst, B. Me, a grown woman, hiding from my ex."

"Not the reunion meeting you were looking for."

"Heck, no."

"Okay. Let's reframe this."

"How?"

"You could see it as romantic instead of humiliating," she offers.

I give her a look. "You're such a PR person, B."

"Okay, not romantic, per se, but definitely heroic in a manly, professional athlete kind of way. He saw you lying on the ground and helped you up." She waggles her brows at me suggestively. "I don't know about you, Kiki, but I'm picturing the guy in red Lycra and a cape right now."

I can't help but giggle at the image, and it ends in a snort.

"Super Dan, hockey god at your service." She gives a salute.

I shake my head. "Why don't you live here permanently, B? I could do with having you around more. Lighten the mood about all things Dan-related."

"I'll be here 'til after the final game. I am happy to lighten everything for you until then."

"It's just ... Oh, I don't know. I guess seeing him again brought back a whole bunch of feelings I had hoped were dead and gone."

She arches a brow at me. "Dead and gone?" she questions, seeing right through me. Blair's one of the few people who knows I still have feelings for Dan after all this time. Blair, Ellie, and my sister, Clara.

"Okay, not dead, exactly. More ... comfortably asleep."

"Why don't you wake up to the hero, then?"

My eyes get huge. "Are you serious right now?" I ask on a chortle. "You know why. He's got this big, exciting life in the spotlight, with those female fans throwing themselves at him at every game. What do they call them?"

"Puck bunnies."

"Terrible name."

She shrugs. "I didn't make it up."

"I can't compete with them. I'm just his high school girlfriend who never did anything with her life."

She leans toward me. "Babe, you've done plenty. Not everyone out there would give up a career to come back and care for their sister and her kids. You're amazing, Kiki, and don't you forget it."

I smile. "You're the best, B."

Everyone needs a Blair in their lives.

I blow out a breath. "I have feelings for a guy I broke up with a lifetime ago, who's not just some regular guy. Oh, no. That would be way too simple. He's a famous NHL star who lives halfway across the country, who probably hasn't given me a second thought since the day he left town, and could have any woman he wants." My shoulders slump. "I'm just going to have to try to avoid him like the plague while he's here. I guess that's all I can do."

"That might be harder than you might think," she replies, her attention focussed on something behind me.

I turn to see the man himself, right here in the bookshop, his bulky hockey-player frame filling the space. He's in a pair of jeans, sneakers, and a hoodie, looking every inch the off-duty athlete that he is. He's looking around the shop, as though searching for something or someone, and when his eyes land on me, my belly does a flip any gymnast would be proud of.

He smiles and lifts a hand to wave before he skirts around a couple of customers, heading to the counter to see his sister. He's accompanied by another big guy, with dark hair and a friendly, handsome face.

Emmy greets her brother with an enthusiastic hug.

Meanwhile, I'm having a minor cardiac arrest.

"You okay there?" Blair asks. "You look like you might want to throw yourself on the ground and hide from the guy again. Which I don't advise, by the way."

"I thought instead of that I might finish my coffee and leave," I reply, draining my cup.

"Kiki, you can't run away every time you see the guy."

"Why not? It seems like a totally plausible approach to me."

Blair gives me a look.

I glance over at Dan and the other guy who are both talking with Emmy. Now is the time to get out of here. I rise to my feet. "Let's get together again soon, okay?"

"Sure thing," she replies, not moving an inch.

"Are you coming with me?"

"I'm meeting my client soon down the street, Mr. Grump. But

you scamper on like the frightened little mouse you are." She waggles her fingers for effect.

Blair has always had an acerbic wit, but right now I could do without it.

I collect my purse, put my head down, and rush toward the exit. Just as I think I'm on safe ground, a large, burly figure steps in my path, blocking my exit.

Dan.

"Where are you rushing off to so quickly?" he asks in that smooth-as-butter voice of his.

"Oh, Dan. Hi. I didn't see you there," I lie. "Did you come in to see your sister? She's so great. I love Emmy. And this shop is amazing. I love it here, but then you know I'm a total book nerd. The coffee is good, too. I just met a friend, but now I've got to go. Places to see and people to do."

I'm babbling worse than a brook.

His lips quirk. "Isn't that 'places to go and people to see'?"

Dang it!

I shrug nonchalantly. "I think you can say it either way, actually."

"Well, you'd know. You've always been the smart one."

I slide my gaze to his before I remember how dangerous it is to look into this man's eyes. I pull my lips into a smile. "I'll let you catch up with your sister." I begin to walk around him.

"Actually, I saw Ellie at the arena today. She's Hannah's teacher these days, right"

"Yup."

"She mentioned you like to come to the bookstore sometimes. Since I was coming here to surprise my sister, I was hoping to bump into you, too."

"Me?" My voice comes out all breathy and full of hope, and I swear my pulse ceases its rhythmic beating for a moment. "What's up?"

"I need to apologize for the other day."

On what planet does *he* need to apologize to *me*?

"You do?"

"Yeah. It was clear I put my foot in it with Benny and the whole hockey thing."

Benny. Right.

"Don't worry about it," I reply with a wave of my hand. "Benny's doing just fine."

I'm not about to tell Dan we can't afford for Benny to play ice hockey as well as for Hannah to have figure skating lessons. Ice hockey is not a cheap sport. Not only are there lessons, but it's all the gear, too. With Clara unable to hold down a job with her health challenges, I'm the sole breadwinner of the household, and although I love my job, it doesn't exactly provide an NHL star's level of income. Not even close.

"I hope you don't mind, but I talked to Ellie about Benny, and she mentioned that there's a team he could join. But she recommended he have some lessons first."

I open my mouth to protest, but he keeps talking.

"She also mentioned that Benny is your nephew, not your son."

My protective shield has been ripped from my hands, leaving me vulnerable. Which is so not where I want to be around this man.

"Oh, you thought that he was my son? How funny," I say on a laugh.

"I did, actually. Crazy, right?"

"Benny and Hannah are Clara's kids. I'm their aunt," I explain, feeling a touch guilty I let him think otherwise. But come on! When it comes to protecting herself, a girl's gotta do what a girl's gotta do.

His face breaks into a knee-weakening smile, and I dig my nails into my palms to stop myself from doing something I may regret. Something like telling him how I feel about him and throwing myself into his arms and kissing his face off.

Not what I need to be doing right now.

"That's what Ellie said. She also said that you bring Hannah to all her lessons."

"Clara can do with the help. She's a single mom these days."

A cloud crosses his features. "Real men don't treat their wives and kids like that, you know. Ellie told me what happened. The guy's scum."

"You don't have to tell me that."

He pauses for a beat before he says, "You're a good person. I hope you know that."

Our gazes lock, and I swear I could get completely lost in the depths of his soft brown eyes.

But I can't let that happen. It will only lead to heartache. He's here for six weeks and then he's gone, back to his big fancy life. And I'll be left behind here in Maple Falls. Again.

I clear my throat. "They're great kids."

"And they're lucky to have you as their aunt."

Would you stop with the compliments? My heart can't take any more!

"The reason I wanted to talk to you is that I'd like to give Benny some hockey lessons. Just to get him started. That way he can get some skills before he tries out for a team."

Could this guy get any sweeter?

I know how much Benny would love that. Not only would he get to learn some basic hockey moves, but being taught by Dan the Man? He would boast about it for years to come.

"Dan, that's so kind of you, but we don't have any of the hockey gear for him."

"Look, I get a whole bunch of stuff for free. It's one of the perks of the job, I guess. I can get him some skates, a helmet, a hockey stick, the whole lot."

"Dan—"

"Let me do this for him, okay? It's no big deal for me. Really."

I can't help but bristle. This might not be a big deal for

someone with his kind of cash, but for us, it's a whole other ball game. "It's a big deal to *me*."

He pulls his lips into a line as he raises one of his big hands in the air. "I'm sorry. That came out wrong. I didn't mean it that way. I meant that I get this free stuff. Benny needs proper hockey skates, so he doesn't hurt himself or others. It's a safety thing."

"Maybe we'll get some second-hand hockey skates."

"Kiki," he says, his tone intimate, familiar. It does weird things to my heart.

"I guess having the right skates can't hurt. I'll talk to Clara about it. You do get them for free, right?"

He grins at me. "I do. Promise." He places his hand over his chest. "He's gonna love learning."

"Oh, I know he will."

"When could you bring him to the arena? We have practice in the mornings, so I'm free most afternoons other than when we have this big media event. Troy said classes are done by five o'clock most days, and I could have the rink for an hour or so then. Would that work for you?"

I study his face, wondering why he's offering to do this. I always knew Dan was a stand-up guy. Back in high school, he was never one of those talented athletes who thought a lot of himself, like some of the other guys. He was a quiet achiever, never boasting, never strutting up and down the hall like he owned the place, like some loud jock who rubbed his prowess in people's faces.

"I'll have to check with his mom," I reply, even though I'm the one who keeps the kids' schedules. I'm trying my best not to fall back in love with him right here among the shelves of books.

A professional hockey player who wants to teach a little boy how to play in his spare time? Dan is yanking on my heartstrings —hard. And the very last thing I need right now is my heartstrings being yanked on by the big NHL star with a glamorous life on the other side of the country.

Dan's face slides into a grin. "Sure. Of course. Let me know."

"Okay. And ... thanks. It's really kind of you."

"If he's half as good a hockey player as his sister is a figure skater, he'll go far." He pulls his latest model iPhone from his pocket. "What's your number?"

"Same as it always was."

"Then you'll still have mine, too."

The fact he's kept my number all these years makes my breath hitch in my throat. That's got to mean something, doesn't it?

I berate myself. I shouldn't go hoping for anything with Dan, even if he's being incredibly sweet and kind in offering to teach Benny.

"I'll call you once you've had a chance to talk to your sister. Is tomorrow good?"

"Tomorrow. Sure."

He holds my gaze for a beat longer than I expect, and my treacherous heart fills with hope, something it seems to want to do whenever he's around.

So much for my avoidance tactic. It's going to prove impossible to avoid Dan now.

CHAPTER 7
DAN

I TIE UP MY SKATES, my wrist reminding me it's still not right. I head out onto the ice, relishing the light wind in my hair as I glide around the rink. It's not often I get to do this—and not at all lately, thanks to my injury. In fact, when I headed out onto the ice with Cooper and Scotty that day I saw Keira, it was the first time I'd skated since Coach informed me I was benched.

I've had a few physical therapy sessions with Jennifer, the team PT, since I've been back here, and she told me I'm definitely on the mend. She saw no harm in me giving Benny a few pointers on the ice. She's even given me the green light to practice with the guys, just as long as I don't do anything to hurt my wrist.

I'm taking it and skating with it. Pun intended.

Today is my first lesson with Benny, and I'm amped to see Keira again. I called her as I had promised, and she told me that her sister was fine with my teaching Benny, and that they could come for their first lesson today.

I was so happy—I punched the air and remained on a high for the rest of the day.

Usually when I'm out on the ice, an arena is full of my teammates. Big personalities and small, talking, skating, being told what to do by Coach. Not today. Practice was over hours ago, and the last of Ellie's class have gone. It's just me, my skates, and the ice, and as I move around the rink, stick in hand, I take a moment to enjoy it before seeing Keira again.

I could have kissed Ellie when she told me that Keira isn't married, and Benny and Hannah are her sister's kids. Of course I didn't. There's only one woman I want to kiss, and she's the one who's held my heart in her hands my entire adult life, only I've been too focused on my hockey career to admit it, even to myself.

Now that I'm sure she's not married to another man, it's not just the gliding across the smooth ice that has me feeling exhilarated. This could be it. This could be my chance with her. My chance to tell her how much she means to me, how I've never forgotten her. How I hope that somehow, if she's willing, we could make this thing between us work once more.

My chests fills with warmth at the possibility.

Me and Kiki, together as one.

It seems so perfect, so *possible*. Sure, my career has always been super important to me, my driving force in life. But seeing Keira again has only served to remind me what I gave up all those years ago.

It was a mistake. A huge mistake. It's one I regret making

every day, especially since I'm confronted with her presence daily.

So, when I saw the opportunity to spend time with Keira by training Benny, I leapt at it. Part of me has always wanted to teach kids someday, to share my skills and passion for the game with the next generation. To inspire them. The fact that Benny also happens to be Keira's nephew? Well, that just adds to the appeal, because let's face it, when you messed up with the love of your life and you get a second chance, you grab it with both hands, and you do not let go.

This could be our rebound play, and I'm not going to let her slip through my fingers.

I need to make her mine again.

I pick up the pace on the ice, my legs finding their rhythm, propelling me faster. The wind whips past my face as I lean into each stride, my muscles working hard. The sensation of speed is intoxicating, a blend of control and wild freedom, and I can't help but grin. I've had my first couple of practices with my team, which have gone as well as you could expect a bunch of guys from opposing teams thrown together could go; we've gotten the big media event done, showing the team off to the world; and now my time is finally my own. I'm free to pursue what—and *who*—I really want.

Keira.

Out of the corner of my eye, a couple of blurred figures captures my attention. I slow my pace, angling my feet to come to a stop beside them, ice shavings spraying.

She's here.

"Hey, guys," I say, my breath coming in short, heavy bursts.

Keira is standing at the side of the rink, holding Benny's hand. Her *nephew's* hand.

That fact still makes me want to punch the air.

She's in the same red jacket from the other day, only this time she's not hiding beneath its hood. Her blonde hair is tied up in a ponytail, her face makeup-free, in stark contrast to so many of the women I meet. She's effortlessly beautiful in a natural, girl-next-door kind of way, and my chest squeezes, just as it does every time I lay eyes on her.

"Dan the Man!" Benny squeals excitedly. "I'm gonna be a hockey player just like you!"

"You sure are, Benny and The Jets," I reply, using Keira's term of endearment for him. "Put it here, dude." I hold out my gloved right hand and he slaps it in a high five, leaping off the ground with impressive athleticism.

I turn my attention to his aunt. "It's good to see you again, Aunt Kiki," I say, teasing.

She smiles at me and it's as though I've won the state lottery.

Man, I have got it so bad for this woman.

"She's not your aunt!" Benny exclaims with a laugh.

"You're right, Benny. My bad."

"Thanks again for doing this," she says. "Clara wanted me to let you know how grateful she is. How grateful we both are."

"You don't need to thank me. I want to do it," I say, my gaze holding hers for a beat, or two, before she looks down.

I turn my attention to Benny. "I've got some skates for you to try on."

"Cool!" Benny exclaims as I step off the ice and onto the floor, showing them where to find the skates.

Ordinarily, I tower over Kiki's 5'6" height, but in my skates, I feel like a giant next to her.

"No need. We brought a pair, so there's no problem." Keira holds up a pair of figure skates. "These were Hannah's. She outgrew them. I know you said he needs hockey skates, but I didn't want to put you out and I haven't had the chance to get some second-hand ones. I figured these will do for now, at least."

"I don't like them. They're girl skates," Benny complains, his bottom lip pushed out in a pout.

"Honey, they still work just the same on the ice." Keira offers them to him, but Benny crosses his arms and looks away.

"May I?" I ask, and Keira nods. Taking them in my hands, I

say, "Benny's got a point, but it's less that they're girl skates and more that they're for figure skating. Remember I told you that hockey skates need to do different things? It's why they have a stiff pad and a curved blade for quick turns. See?" I point at my own skates. "Figure skates have ankle support for jumps and spins, with a longer, flatter blade."

"See, Aunt Kiki? I told you," says Benny.

Keira's face colors. "These are all we've got," she says to me quietly, and although I know she's embarrassed, I admit I love the intimacy in her soft, feminine voice.

"That's why I got some hockey skates for him. We talked about this, and I thought you were okay with it?" I ask, hoping I haven't overstepped the mark again.

This feels like a minefield.

"I remember."

"If it's a problem—"

"No. It's fine," she replies, pulling her lips into a smile.

"I want the skates. Real hockey skates, not dumb figure-skating ones," Benny says, and Keira's eyes flash to mine.

"Only if it's okay with Aunt Kiki," I reply.

She pauses for a beat before she replies, "It's okay. Thank you, Dan."

I grin. "Do you want to try some on?" I ask Benny. "I've got a bunch of kids sizes because I didn't know which to get."

Keira finds the right size from my embarrassingly large selection, and then she helps him into a pair of lightly padded ski pants, so that when he inevitably falls on the ice, he'll at least be cushioned.

"When do I get to wear the pads?" Benny asks as Keira ties up his laces.

"Benny's always wanted to run before he can walk," she says with a laugh.

"We'll get to the gear soon enough. First, you gotta learn how to skate, buddy. Have you been on the ice before?"

"Sure! I'm a pro," Benny declares, his self-confidence making me smile.

"Just your regular free-for-all skating," Keira qualifies. "I've brought him here a few times, usually around Christmas. Troy holds these sessions with Christmas tunes and a big tree over by the office. It's really festive and fun. He can stand and move well enough. Right, Benny?"

"Right," he replies.

"That sure sounds like a pro to me. Okay, buddy, let's get out there, shall we?"

Benny throws his fists in the air. "Yeah!"

"But here's a helmet. Safety first." I slide a helmet onto his head before I slip my own helmet back on and clip it into place.

"This is so kind of you, Dan," Keira says, and I notice how her gray-blue eyes look particularly iridescent today. "But you've got to let me pay you for the lesson. It's the least I can do."

I wave her words away. "I told you: I want to do this."

"I insist, Dan. I can't afford your NHL-level fees of course, but you've got to at least let me pay you something."

I land on an idea. "Tell you what, you can buy me a hot chocolate after."

She looks over at the counter where a member of staff is working the hot chocolate machine for a customer. Turning her gaze back at me, she shrugs. "That'll be one big hot chocolate."

I let out a laugh. "Sounds great to me. I always used to love the hot chocolates here after a game back in the day."

I shared those hot chocolates with her. I wonder if she's remembering that, too.

"Come on, Dan the Man," Benny calls impatiently from the ice.

"Do you want to join us?" I ask her.

She holds her book up. "Heathcliff has almost got his revenge."

"Are you sure? If you didn't bring any skates, you know I've got a bunch over here." I gesture at the collection.

She looks like she might waver for a moment before she reaffirms her resolve. "You guys go have fun. I'm going to sit here and try to work out why Heathcliff is considered a romantic hero, because I'm not seeing it right now."

"Okay."

That's one of the things I have always loved the most about Keira. She doesn't take things at face value. She wants to understand. She investigates, wanting to know, wanting to learn. "A thirst for knowledge" is the way our twelfth grade English teacher, Mrs. Nelson, described it, and it would seem she's not lost it, ten years on.

Although I could stand and talk to Keira all day, I've got a lesson to give to Benny, so I tear myself away from her and head out onto the ice, holding a kid-size hockey stick. When I reach Benny's side, I hand it to him, watching as his eyes light up.

"For me?" he asks.

"For you. To keep."

He holds it up in the air. "Look, Aunt Kiki! I got my own hockey stick!"

"You're so lucky!" Keira calls back. "Did you thank Dan?"

"Thanks, Dan," Benny says immediately.

"Shall I show you how to use it?"

"I already know," he insists and proceeds to skate, holding his stick in front of him with one hand, about a foot above the ice.

Points for enthusiasm, but not so much for technique.

"How about I show you the proper grip? Both hands. Top hand controls, bottom hand guides."

He grips it, his eyes wide with the novelty.

"Nice work, Benny. Now, why don't you feel the puck with the stick?" I slide a puck from my pocket onto the ice in front of him.

He fumbles at first, his stick awkwardly chasing the puck like a cat after a laser pointer, barely making contact.

"The trick is to keep it close, like it's attached to the end of your stick," I advise him.

He nods, focused on the task. With a few more tries, he's pushing the puck along, a little more confidently each time.

"Nice work! You'll be deking out goalies in the NHL in no time," I say.

"What's deking?" he asks.

"It's short for decoy and it means you trick an opposing player out of their position so you can get past them and score a goal."

"I wanna do that," he replies with a grin.

"Kid, we all wanna do that," I tell him with a laugh. "Watch this."

I drop another puck from my pocket onto the ice and push it around. I pull back to shoot for goal and as my stick makes contact with the puck, a jolt of hot, searing pain shoots up my left arm from my wrist.

"Ah!" I utter reflexively, dropping my stick to grip my wrist.

Benny looks at me in confusion. "I don't think that's how you do it," he says, his brows pulled inward, making him look like a serious adult.

I can't help but laugh despite the pain.

"Dan! Are you all right?" Keira calls from the sideline.

I turn to look at her and give her the thumbs up. "Just being dramatic." I tell Benny to practice his moves and skate over to her.

"It's your wrist, right? I heard you had an injury."

"I was dumb. The PT told me not to overdo it, but I got carried away trying to show Benny how to shoot for a goal."

"You've got to take care of yourself," she says, and the concern in her voice fills my chest with a warm glow.

"I'll try."

We share a smile, and it feels as though I am one step closer to my goal of making her mine once more.

"Dan! Look at me!" Benny calls out, and I turn to see him nudging the puck into the goal from a five-foot distance.

"Awesome work, Benny," I say.

His smile says it all—this could be the beginning of something great for him, and I'm happy to come along for the ride.

"I'll give him another ten minutes or so," I say to Keira.

"As long as your wrist is okay?" Her brow is furrowed with worry, and I can't help but smile.

"It's fine, but thanks for checking." My wrist gives a contrary throb, but right now, basking in Keira's smile, I could not care less.

I try a few more moves with Benny before time's up. Together, we skate back to the edge of the rink where Keira is waiting for us.

"You looked great out there, champ," Keira says as Benny flops down beside her.

"It was so fun. Dan's the best. He said I'm gonna make it to the NHL."

"Keep up the great work you put in today and you'll have a shot," I reply.

"Well, how about we focus on one lesson at a time for now and then see how things go?" Keira suggests, clearly tempering her nephew's lofty aspirations.

"Speaking of which, is the day after tomorrow for his next lesson okay with you? Same time?" I try to keep the eagerness from my voice. Fail.

"I don't want to use up too much of your time."

"You're not. Trust me."

"But what about practices and all the things you've got to do with the team? Publicity and such, and spending time with Emmy and your parents, not to mention Mimi? You must be super busy."

"I've got a few things coming up, but practice is in the mornings, and other than spending time with my family, I'm as free as a bird."

She shoots me an uncertain look. I get why. She feels indebted to me, her ex. But what she doesn't know is that I'll do anything to get close to her, and besides, teaching Benny has been a lot of fun. It feels good to give back to a kid from my hometown with the same dreams as I once had.

"What about your wrist? The last thing we want to do is set you back. The whole town is counting on you leading this team to victory."

"Do you have any more arguments to throw at me for me not to teach your nephew?"

I can almost see the cogs in her brain turning over. "Look, Benny's got a lot of promise. He picked the skills up pretty fast out there. Plus, he's a great kid."

She smiles, looking down at her nephew who has removed his skates, the love she has for him palpable. "He sure is."

"So that's set then. The day after tomorrow, same time." She opens her mouth to say something, and I add, "I want to do this for him."

And I want to be close to you.

"Thanks," she replies.

"Now, how about that hot chocolate you promised me?"

Her lips lift into a smile that brightens her whole face. "One hot chocolate, coming up. Do you want one, too, Benny?"

"Hot chocolate!" he says, bouncing up and down on the spot.

She shakes her head in good humor at her nephew. "I'll take that as a yes."

We order our hot chocolates and sit in the bleachers to drink them. We ordered extra marshmallows, mainly for the delicious goo factor, and as Keira takes her first sip, she gets a marshmallow moustache. It takes all my strength not to lean in and kiss it right off, savoring the sweet taste of the marshmallow—and her.

I know it's way too soon, but a man wants what a man

wants. And this man wants the woman sitting next to me looking so sexy and adorable with a marshmallow moustache.

"This is nice. Like old times," I say.

"It is," she replies.

"Aunt Kiki's got a mustache!" Benny teases, and her eyes wide with embarrassment; she quickly wipes her top lip.

"Personally, I thought it suited you," I say and win a laugh from her.

"You could have told me." She nudges me with her shoulder, and it strikes me that this is our first physical touch since we broke up. It's a small thing, but I see it as a definite step in the right direction.

"How's Mimi doing? Emmy told me she lives with her these days to help out."

"We're all super grateful to Emmy. Mimi's arthritis is causing her some trouble, but you know Mimi: nothing much keeps her down."

My grandmother is a force to be reckoned with. An indomitable spirit, she won't let something as trifling as painful arthritis get in the way of living her life to the fullest. Having Emmy live with her has helped a lot, and I'm grateful to know my sister is keeping a close eye on her these days. We all are.

"She's one of the reasons I grabbed the chance to come back here to play for the Ice Breakers. She's not getting younger, and time with her is special."

"I love Mimi. She sometimes comes to the farmers' market on the weekends, and I see her chatting with the townsfolk, always with a smile on her face. Give her my best when you next see her?"

"Of course I will. You run the Maple Falls Farmers' Market, right?"

Her face lights up with a fresh smile. "I do. I love it. The stall holders are great, and I get to enjoy live music each day as I do my job. Plus, I am given a bunch of fresh produce each weekend, which means Benny and Hannah have to eat their vegetables."

I chuckle. "I bet they're super happy about that."

"You know kids and vegetables."

Benny is now pretending to hit an imaginary puck with his hockey stick against the carpet, giving a commentary on his seemingly endless ability to score goal after goal.

"Do you really think he's got promise?" Keira asks.

"I wouldn't have said it if I didn't think it. No point getting the kid's hopes up for no reason."

"He's wanted to be a hockey player since he came to his first game when he was only three. But hockey's an expensive sport. I remember your family having to make sacrifices to allow you to pursue your dreams."

"My dad worked as many extra shifts at the gas station, after his regular work day, as he could get," I reply, remembering how incredible my parents were in their support of me and my chosen career path. Dad had his nine to five at the lumber mill, and while Mom was running me around to lessons and practices, he would pull shifts at the gas station over on 3rd Street. But he'd always manage to be at my games, come what may, with him and Mom in the bleachers, cheering me on.

Everyone knew it was a gamble. The stats say it all: fewer than five percent of high school hockey players make it into the NHL. I may be pointing out the obvious, but that's over ninety-five percent who don't. The odds sure were stacked against me. But my parents believed in me, and they did what they could to help me realize my dream.

That's just the way they're built. They supported all us kids with our chosen paths: me with hockey, Ethan with acting, and Emmy with her love of all things books.

Although I know I can never truly thank them for everything they did for me, I can show them in the small ways available to me now. I offered to buy them a new house at the wealthier end of town, a new-build with all the modern conveniences, but they wanted to stay in their home. So instead, I paid off their mortgage for them, a fact they thank me for repeatedly every time we see one another, no matter how many times I tell them they don't need to thank me at all.

I take in Keira's tight-lipped frown. "Is everything okay?" I ask.

She takes a deep breath. "I'm going to level with you, Dan. You're super kind to offer Benny hockey gear, but one day he will grow out of those, and then we'll have to buy new ones, and the pattern will repeat until he's fully grown if he really wants to pursue hockey. As generous as you are, I think it's only going to be hard for him when we can't allow him to keep playing."

"I know exactly what you're talking about. But please, let me take care of it."

She shakes her head. "I wouldn't feel comfortable doing that."

I land on an idea. "This charity we're here playing for is a kids' charity. The Happy Horizons Ranch. Angel Davis runs it. I could see what she could do for Benny."

And if they can't help him, I'll make it happen. I just won't tell Keira.

"I don't think they give money to kids wanting to play ice hockey," she replies with a light laugh. "It's a ranch where Angel and her team help kids learn outdoor and farming skills. That kind of thing."

"Got it. I'll work something out. Leave it to me?"

What's the point of all the money I get for shooting a puck around on a rink if I can't use it to help the people I love?

Okay, *like*. The people I like. Only, when it comes to Keira, it sure feels a whole lot more like love.

Ellie walks past, noticing us sitting on the bleachers together, and comes to a stop, smiling up at us. "It's just like old times, you two here together."

I steal a glance at Keira. She's smiling, looking a little awkward—and a whole lot beautiful.

"We're catching up over a hot chocolate, that's all," Keira replies. "Dan just gave Benny a private hockey lesson."

"So I hear." She raises her brows at me as though she doesn't know about it. "Is that a service you're offering all the kids in Maple Falls now that you're back, Dan?"

I know she's teasing—and fishing. Definitely fishing.

"I'd be happy to," I reply smoothly.

"Tell you what. I'll keep it a secret, so you're not mobbed by all the kids in town." She throws us a wink. "Have fun, you two," she says before she walks away.

I steal a look at Keira. Her cheeks are glowing, lighting up her beautiful face, and I allow myself the hope that maybe, over time, she'll remember how good it was to be with me. And she'll want me back, just as much as I want her.

CHAPTER 8
KEIRA

I SLAM the car door shut, balancing two overstuffed paper grocery bags in my arms. Jonelle, a woman who runs one of the fresh produce stalls at the farmers' market gave me a pumpkin and a recipe for pie that doesn't involve using canned pumpkin puree. So, tonight I plan on making a pumpkin pie from scratch for the family, making the pastry gluten-free for Clara. I'm not exactly a born baker, but I do love a good pumpkin pie in fall, and since I'm the only one in the house who could make one, it's up to me to pull out my best Martha Stewart. And if using Jonelle's pumpkin proves too hard, I've got some backup canned puree in the kitchen pantry—I just won't tell Jonelle.

Snow begins to fall, and I look up at the darkening sky in surprise. Snow? In fall? That hardly ever happens. The kids are going to love it. I take a moment the let the small flakes land on my face, melting on impact, before I begin to climb the steps up to the house. I'm so busy thinking about snow and Dan—okay, mainly about Dan—when I put my weight on the broken step and almost fall flat on my face, crashing to the floor. Apples go rolling across the porch, and a mandarin orange is propelled toward the front door with a smack, landing in a moist mess on the welcome mat.

Dang it! I have *got* to fix that step.

If only there were enough time in the day.

I collect the errant groceries, telling myself to clean up the mandarin, and pushing through the door, I call out to Benny. He's got his next lesson with Dan this afternoon, and last time we were late. It's not a good look. Dan's doing this as a favor for us, and we need to respect his time.

Plus, I'll admit, being late suggests I'm not totally in control of my life, which I'm trying desperately to show him I am. Poised, in control, crushing it. That's the goal. Not tripping on steps I should have fixed months ago, bruising apples and propelling mandarins.

As I make my way into the house, I glance down the hallway and to my surprise, Benny appears at the entrance to his and Hannah's room, wearing his thick tracksuit pants, his warm jacket, and holding his hockey stick in his hands with his helmet on his head.

"Wow, Benny. You're all set?" I ask him in wonderment. Anyone who has ever cared for a six-year-old boy will know just how miraculous this moment is.

"He's been wearing his hockey clothes for the last hour, waiting for you," Hannah informs me from behind her brother. "He's in *love* with hockey."

"Am not," Benny states.

"Are too," Hannah counters. "You love hockey. You want to kiss it."

"No, I don't!" Benny insists.

"Yeah, you do. You want to kiss it. You want to love it. You want to—"

"No!" Benny insists. "Aunt Kiki, tell her I don't want to kiss hockey."

"Hannah," I warn, still balancing the groceries in my arms. "You're being unkind about something that's super important to your brother."

"Yeah, Hannah," Benny echoes.

I hear Clara calling me from the living room. "Coming!" I call out before I give a stern look to the kids. "Be nice to each other."

"I am being nice," Benny harrumphs. "And you want to kiss figure skating."

"You're right," Hannah says smugly.

I roll my eyes. *Kids.*

"Did you know it's started snowing out there?" I ask to distract them.

It works. Their eyes bulge and immediatly, they rush to the closest window to see.

I push the swing door to the living room open with my back. "I got the apples you wanted but tripped on that dang step again and—" I trail off as I take in Clara sitting up on the sofa, a beaming smile on her face, and I look from her to the person sitting on one of the chairs.

Dan.

My breath catches in my throat.

Immediately he's on his feet, taking the bags of groceries from me, and throwing me one of his knee-weakening smiles. "Let me take those from you. You tripped on a step? Are you all right?"

"Dan," I reply breathlessly. "Wh-what are you doing here?"

"Now, Kiki, is that any way to greet our guest?" Clara asks, her eyes teasing.

Just what I need to make me look poised and in control of my wonderful, exciting life: my big sister telling me what to do in front of Dan.

"My sister's right," I concede. "It's nice to see you… here … in our living room."

So smooth.

His lips quirk. "It's great to be here … in your living room."

Is he teasing me? One look into his eyes confirms it.

"It brings back a lot of memories being here," he continues.

"I bet it does. Great memories, I imagine," says my sister, who suddenly seems not to be suffering from CFS at all and is instead super perky.

I shoot her a look that I hope tells her she's stirring the pot and she needs to stop, *now*.

But instead, she continues, that metaphorical wooden spoon held firmly in her hands as she stirs away. "What do you remember exactly, Dan? I'm eager to know. Aren't you eager to know, Kiki?"

Still stirring the pot, Clara.

"I remember dinners here," he replies.

"But that's not all, right? I bet you remember Kiki's room, with all those One Direction posters on her walls?"

I think my sister just earned a gold medal in pot stirring.

I'm not biting. Instead, I ask, "How about I show you where to put those grocery bags, Dan?"

"That would be great," he replies.

"Right this way."

Clara is still grinning, and I throw her another look as I lead Dan from the living room to the kitchen. Being older, our house is not open plan like so many, and there's a swing door that leads from the dining room that we use as a playroom for the kids, into the kitchen. I push through it, holding it open for him.

Dan puts the groceries where I tell him before he turns back to face me, leaning against the kitchen counter, his large, masculine bulk filling the room in a way none of us do. He looks about as relaxed as I feel tense. But then we always were polar opposites. The jock and the nerd.

"I'm sorry about Clara. She doesn't get out much, so we're her only entertainment," I say.

Those way-too sexy lips of his quirk into another smile. "You don't have Netflix?" he asks, and I know it's his turn to tease me.

"You know what I mean. Anyway, at the risk of sounding rude once more, I thought we were meeting you at the arena for Benny's lesson."

"I figured I could drop by here with some things for you before we do that. I hope that's okay?"

"Of course. But if it's more hockey gear for Benny—"

He raises his hands in surrender. "It's for everyone. Fan merch for the Ice Breakers team. We got an allocated amount and I figured I'd give a bunch away to the people I know."

"You know everyone in this town, Dan."

"I know, but you're top of my list."

I try not to let a flush of happiness show in my face. "Well, Benny will be super excited to get some Ice Breakers merchandise."

"I figured as much."

"What are you two doing in there? Do I need to chaperone?" Clara calls out, and I make a mental note to have some seriously stern words with my trouble-causing older sister once Dan leaves. I don't need to be teased about the man I've never gotten over, particularly not in my own home.

I chance a look at Dan. He's watching me as though he is gauging my reaction, looking ridiculously hot in his form-fitting T-shirt that more than hints at his muscular arms and torso beneath.

"Do we need a chaperone?" he asks, his voice soft and quiet. It does things to my being. Things I can't allow to happen, not if I'm going to keep myself safe from this man. But oh, how easy it would be to forget all that and instead step into his big arms and get lost in his embrace, dissolving into a kiss.

I toss my hair and raise my chin, pushing any such thoughts away.

Not helpful.

But really, that was definitely a little flirtatious. Wasn't it? Which would mean that Dan is standing in my kitchen, flirting with me. And if he is flirting with me, what does that mean? Does it mean that he's interested in me? That he still has feelings for me?

That he still loves me?

My breath pitches in my throat.

But I've got to push any and all such wild assumptions aside. Dan has moved on. He's a famous NHL star. He has women throwing themselves at him every day of his life. What would he want, flirting with the girl he left behind?

The door to the kitchen swings open and in bursts Benny, his hockey stick in hand, his helmet still on his head. "Watch me, Dan!" he insists as he nudges an imaginary puck across the kitchen floor. "I'm shooting for a goal!" He swings his hockey stick up and hits the imaginary puck into an imaginary goal by the oven, his hockey stick banging up against the metal with a *clang*.

"Benny! Be careful," I scold, inspecting the oven for damage. It may be ancient, but it still works, and we can't afford a new one. "Maybe it's best you take that stick out to the yard."

"But the yard is covered in grass, not ice," he complains.

"The kitchen floor isn't ice either, buddy," I reply. "We've talked about using your hockey stick in the house before."

Benny lowers his head. "I know."

"What's the rule?" I ask.

"But I just wanted to show Dan and he hasn't been here before." He pauses before he adds, "And it's snowing out there." As though that would be the clincher in his argument.

"It's my fault. I told him to be ready to go when I arrived, which evidently meant practice with his hockey stick inside." He makes the long trip to crouch down to Benny's height, quite a ways for a guy the size of Dan. "How about we save your skills for the ice, pal? Follow your aunt's rules."

"Okay," Benny says immediately, and I look at Dan in wonder as he pulls open the back door and takes his stick out to the yard.

"Remind me to get you over here whenever Benny is pushing back, which is most days," I say.

"I'm at your service," Dan replies with a little bow, as though he's a gentleman in *Bridgerton*.

Don't think of Dan as a gentleman in Bridgerton. That will do absolutely nothing to dispel the way I feel about him. Nothing at all.

Too late, my mind leaps on the idea, picturing Dan on the show, all swagger and confidence, shooting me sizzling looks across a ballroom floor.

I blow out a breath.

"Shall we go back to see Clara?" I ask. I don't wait for his reply, instead turning on my heel and pushing through the kitchen door. Being alone in the kitchen with him is dangerous territory, particularly with my newly minted *Bridgerton*-obsessed mind.

Netflix has a lot to answer for.

"Hi again, you two," Clara says lightly as we re-enter the living room. "Dan, why don't you show Kiki what you brought for us?"

Hannah is now sitting at the little table and chairs by the window, studiously coloring, as she loves to do. Dan opens a backpack resting against the wall by the door.

"We've got the first game coming up soon and I wanted to give you all these," he says as he passes me a plastic-wrapped parcel. "It's an Ice Breakers jersey. I brought one for everyone."

"Isn't that kind?" Clara says.

Hannah looks up from her coloring. "Do I get one too, Dan?"

"You sure do. Catch." He throws a jersey to Hannah, who catches it in both hands.

I pull the plastic off and hold the jersey up. It's mostly white with light blue accents, at the collar and cuffs. The sleeves have bold red stripes running across them, and there's a matching red stripe across the chest. The center features a logo with "Ice Breakers" written in bold letters, surrounded by a graphic of a shattered ice puck.

"Aren't they great?" Clara asks. "I've already got mine on." She pulls the blanket from her shoulders to reveal the same jersey as I'm holding in my hands. "I put it on while you were in the kitchen, *unchaperoned*."

Nope, I'm still not going to bite. I'm too busy reading the number and name on the back of the jersey.

29. *Roberts*.

I look from the jersey up into Dan's eyes. He's smiling at me, his eyes soft, just the way I remember them back when we were dating in high school. He had a way of looking at me that made me feel safe, like I was the most important person in the world to him. He's giving me that look right now, and it takes me back to the way we were when we were one another's everything, the way I always thought we'd be together, even after we broke up.

What did I know?

"It's your number," I murmur, my throat dry.

"It's your birthday. February ninth," he confirms.

If ever I was looking for a clear sign that Dan feels the same way about me as I do about him, this is it. At least that's what I'm telling myself for the minute. I'm sure I'll talk myself out of it pretty soon as it would be too good to be true. My birth date as his number.

"But—" I'm totally lost for words. It's such a sweet gesture. Bold, in fact. He's telling everyone that he remembers me. That I was important to him. That perhaps I'm important to him still.

"I hope you'll wear it," he says.

"Of course she'll wear it! Aunt Kiki loves you!" Hannah says, and my heart leaps into my mouth as I turn and gawk at her.

How?

When?

What?!

I glance at my sister. Clara's eyes are the size of our dinner plates, just as I bet mine are, too.

"Wh-what did you say?" I stutter, barely hearing my words over the thudding of my heart.

I don't look at Dan.

"You love him," Hannah says simply.

I blink at her in shock. Is this one of those "out of the mouths of babes" situations here, or is my niece way more emotionally astute than I've ever given her credit?

"What do you mean, honey?" Clara asks.

Hannah looks between us. "Aunt Kiki loves Dan," she repeats, shrugging, and if the ground could swallow me whole right about now, I'd be very grateful. "Everyone loves Dan the Man," she clarifies.

I hadn't even realized I was holding my breath until air comes whooshing out of my lungs in utter relief. Hannah doesn't know anything about how I feel about Dan, and she hasn't just blurted my innermost secret to the one man who can never know how I really feel.

Unless … I look down at the number on the jersey in my hands. *Unless he feels it too?*

"You're our hometown hero. That's what Ms. Marshall said at school," Hannah continues. "She said everyone will be wearing your number at the first game because we all love you."

"You've got that right, honey," Clara says, darting me a look.

Benny comes crashing into the room, his stick whacking against the door frame.

"Benny! You are going to devalue this house the way you're going," Clara complains, but she's got a big smile on her face as Dan hands him a jersey, which he rips from its plastic with glee.

"Number 29!" he says.

Dan chuckles. "Do you think you could wear it to the first game?"

"I'm gonna wear it all the time," Benny replies, discarding his winter jacket on the floor and throwing the jersey on.

I stand, rooted to the spot, my mind darting around the possibilities. Why would Dan do something as sweet as making his number my birthday if he didn't feel something for me?

My pulse is galloping so fast and loud in my ears I'm surprised no one else can hear it. My mouth has gone dry, and as I look up at Dan, he smiles back at me with such sincerity and warmth, I feel as though I'm floating.

"Oh, would you look at you two kids. Don't you look terrific in your jerseys?" Clara exclaims, looking happier than I've seen her in a long time.

"Yes, thank you. For all of this," I say.

"You're welcome," he murmurs, and for the first time I allow myself to hope.

CHAPTER 9
DAN

MAPLE FEST HAS ALWAYS BEEN the biggest annual event in my hometown. I have such fond memories of the parade, the pumpkin carving contest, the little dogs in costume, gorging myself silly on maple popcorn and maple fried dough, not to mention the cotton candy that mom always said would rot my teeth. I didn't care, I was a kid, sucking every last drop of fun out of the annual town fall festival.

Then, when I got older, I would hang out at the festival with the other guys on the ice hockey team. I would pretend to be as cool as they were, all of us big guys attracting attention from the girls. But me? Well, I only had eyes for one girl. Yup, I was in love with Keira Johnson way before she even spoke to me.

Tragic, right? I prefer to think of it as romantic. I was a fourteen-year-old guy, a jock, popular with guys and girls alike, and all I could do was think about the mysterious girl with her nose buried in a book.

And then, when I finally plucked up the courage to talk to her when I was sixteen—I was not a fast mover—somehow I found the words to ask her out, and she stunned me by saying yes.

Our first date was to Maple Fest. As we wandered around with my teammates and their girlfriends, I slung my arm around her shoulders. It felt incredible to get to be so close to her after wanting to be with her for so long. We meandered through the festivities, drinking maple apple cider and feeling very grown up, in the evening under the lights, strung overhead.

It was the most romantic thing I'd ever seen in my short life.

Of course, there was the hayride, that seminal, almost cliché, small-town experience. I had just turned sixteen and Keira was still fifteen when we first hopped onboard. Shy and awkward, it felt good to be away from my jock friends, who'd been teasing me mercilessly about dating the nerd. I didn't care. They could have their cheerleaders and popular girls, with their highlighted hair, makeup, and short skirts. I wanted Keira.

We sat side by side, my nerves pinging about me like balls in a pinball machine. I reached for her hand, the touch of her soft skin sending a jolt of electricity through me. And then, when I finally plucked up the courage, with my pulse hammering in my chest like a drum machine, I cupped her face in my hand, leaned in toward her, and softly brushed my lips against hers.

Our first kiss.

She had smiled up at me, her face a rosy pink, and I knew she felt it too.

We were inseparable after that.

As I think back on those days, I didn't know how good I had it. As crazy in love with Keira as I was, I figured it would always be like that with women. I didn't know how special it was. I took it for granted, assuming after I left for college that I would meet someone new when I was older and ready to settle down, fall in love with that same feeling I had whenever I was around Keira: that heady combination of hot, molten desire and the innate knowledge, held deep within my very bones, that I loved her.

I walk past the stalls selling cotton candy and cider and spot my teammate, Cooper Montgomery. With his perpetual frown in place, he's standing mute as his PR person, Blair, I think he said her name was, talks to him. He looks about as happy about whatever it is she's saying to him as he does about pretty much everything.

I throw him a smile as I make my way toward the team table. Some of the guys from the Ice Breakers are already here, signing jerseys and other Ice Breakers merch, chatting with the townsfolk and visitors. Ted "the Bear" Powell; Dawson Hayes, my old college buddy and teammate; and Noah Beaumont, the former hot property of the NHL, brought back to earth with his relegation to the AHL a while back, are talking at the team table with a group of people I don't recognize.

I slide in beside them. "Hey, guys," I say, and Dawson reaches out and gives me a fist bump.

"Watch out, guys. Maple Falls' favorite son is here. We're about to get mobbed," Dawson says as he flashes me a grin.

I shrug. "What can I say? I can't help that everyone loves me."

"Yeah, I'm sure it's a real drag for you," he replies.

"What's up, Dan?" Ted says with a lift of his chin.

"Hey," I reply before I take my seat and grab a pen, a line of people forming in front of me. Several move from Ted's line to me, and he shrugs and shakes his head at me good-naturedly.

Cooper sits down heavily in a chair on my other side and wryly observes the growing crowd. "Why don't they have a statue of you? I half expected one when I went downtown," he says, and I think he's making a joke, but it isn't clear.

"It's just cause I'm the hometown guy," I reply.

"You're our hometown hero," Marie-Ellen McCluskey, the resident town gossip, says as she thrusts a jersey with my number on it in front of me.

"Hey, Mrs. McCluskey. Nice to see you," I say as I scrawl my signature across the jersey.

"Put some kisses on it," she instructs.

I glance up at her. She looks just the same as she did when I lived here: cropped grey hair, glasses, her lined face lifted in a big smile. "Sure thing." I add a couple of kisses in the form of "x" to the jersey and hand it to her.

"Now everyone in my knitting circle will be jealous," she says.

Dawson shakes his head. "Man, you're like a God in these parts. I wonder if anyone will be wearing a jersey that *doesn't* have the number twenty-nine on it at the games."

The mention of my number makes me think of Keira. Heck, most things make me think of Keira now that I'm back in Maple Falls. And particularly since I'm here at Maple Fest, memories of us together are my constant companions.

The way she looked at me when I gave her my jersey and explained my number sends a warm glow spreading through me, like sunlight breaking through the clouds. It gave me hope, and if we hadn't left straight away for Benny's lesson, and I hadn't needed to leave from the arena to go to dinner at my parents' place, I would have tried to get her alone and finally found the courage to tell how I feel about her.

I hope to get that chance soon. Real soon.

"Look out, guys. Puck bunnies at eleven o'clock. And they're all Dan Roberts fans," Dawson says, gesturing at a group of women wearing my jersey. One of them has it knotted at the front, exposing her taut belly, and as her eyes land on me she tosses her long dark hair and throws me a flirty smile.

"Definitely puck bunnies," Cooper grinds out, sounding totally unimpressed by them.

The women reach the desk, and a couple of them begin to flirt with all of us. The one with the long dark hair has me in her sights, and she leans on the table toward me, her hair falling over one eye.

"It's great to see you again, Dan," she purrs.

"I'm sorry. Do I know you?" I ask, not recognizing her.

"We met in Chicago after a game last winter. I'm Lana. My friend, Stacey, and I talked to you for ages at Glenn's party?" she replies, referring to the Blizzard's defenseman, Glenn Mitchell.

I vaguely remember the party—one of many, I'm sure. There are always parties after matches when you play in the NHL, particularly if your team wins. And with the parties come the women. Plenty of them.

"My friend, Stacey, got on real well with Glenn that night," Lana continues. "And I thought you and I got on pretty well, too."

Now that I look at her, I do remember her from that party at Glenn's house, just down the road from my own. A few of us had houses in the same neighborhood, and we often hung out together between practices. When you're a recognizable face it's often easier to hang with the team rather than navigate others. Sometimes it's hard to know who's genuine and who's not, and I've found I can trust my teammates.

The way Lana toyed with her hair the whole time we talked comes back to me, her shirt tied in the same knot, exposing her midriff. She was flirting, making it clear what her intentions were toward me, and I'd been tempted, I'll admit. She's a gorgeous, sexy woman and I was single. But I've never been one to go for the puck bunnies much, not like some of my teammates. They're only interested in you because you're in the NHL.

That might have been enough when I first started out, but it got old, real fast.

"How are you doing, Lana? Sorry I didn't recognize you straight away." I glance at her empty hands. "Have you got something for me to sign?"

"This shirt," she replies, straightening up so I get the full view of her figure, showcased in her skintight pants and cropped shirt. "Right about here." She points at her chest.

Subtle? That would be a hard *no*.

Dawson throws me a knowing look.

I lift my lips into a fake smile. "No can do, sorry, Lana, but if you get a new jersey from over there," I gesture at the merch stand. "I'll sign that one for you, no problem."

Her features drop, but I'm no longer looking at Lana. I spot Keira, talking with Cooper's PR person. She's laughing at something she said, her whole face lit up. Unlike the walking sex advertisement in front of me, Keira is wearing a fall-appropriate jacket, fully covering her midriff, over a pair of jeans and sneakers, a bobble hat on top of her head.

She looks cute and sexy in a much more subtle way than women like Lana. My chest expands at the sight of her.

She looks in my direction and I raise a hand in greeting. She flashes me her slightly shy smile before she returns her attention to her friend.

"Oh, you could do so much better than *her*," Lana says, clearly having watched Keira's and my exchange. "Although I guess she's cute in that kind of girl-next-door kind of way. I could totally rock that look, you know. Just give me the word."

I'll give her points for persistence.

One of the younger guys on the Ice Breakers team, a twenty-one-year-old kid called Nate who looks a lot like an oversized Thor, plunks down next to Cooper. "Better late than never, right?" he says with a grin in Lana's direction.

I see an opportunity.

"Nate, meet my old friend, Lana," I say.

He stretches out his hand and takes hers. "Nathaniel Simpson, although you can call me Nate."

She glances down at his jersey. "You're on the team?"

"Babe, I *am* the team," he replies, and I swear I see Lana melt on the spot.

I seize the opportunity to escape.

"I'll be back in a few," I tell the guys.

"You only just got here, man," Dawson complains.

"Yeah, but I gotta see about a girl," I tell him, and he raises his brows at me in question.

"I'll tell you another time," I say as I see Keira hugging Blair and turning to walk away.

In a few short strides I catch up to her. "Kiki," I say, and she turns and looks at me.

"Dan. I thought you were signing merchandise," she replies, and I hope against all things holy that she didn't see Lana flirting with me. Not that I flirted back of course, but I'm sure it didn't look good to have a woman leaning in close to me, dressed the way she was.

"I'm done with that," I tell her, even though I'm not officially done. I take a mental note to apologize to Coach Strickland later. But there are some things that are more important than signing jerseys. "I thought we could hang out a while. Like old times."

"I was just going to check on the pumpkin carving. I provided all the pumpkins, you see. It's my thing."

"Pumpkins?"

Her lips quirk into a smile. "I'm involved in the whole setup with the pumpkins for the Maple Fest."

"Got it. Are you running the pumpkin carving these days?"

"Actually, I'm involved in the whole festival. I guess it goes with the territory when you run the town's farmers' market."

I throw an admiring glance over her. She's become so enmeshed in our town, become such a part of it.

Is it terrible that I feel a pang of jealousy?

Yup. Terrible. I can't seriously be jealous of a town, even if I want all of her attention on me.

We reach the pumpkin carving area where there are a bunch of pumpkins already carved on a shelf, people working hard at their creations with tub loads of pumpkins ready and waiting for people's artistic endeavors. I spot a few people I know, including Harlow Lemieux, the woman Ted insists he's "just good friends" with, and say hello to them as Keira checks up on the status.

"Daniel Roberts," a voice says, and I look down to see Mrs. Nelson, my old high school English teacher, holding a carved pumpkin in her hands.

"Hello, Mrs. Nelson. Nice to see you again. Great work you got there."

"Oh, this?" She holds the pumpkin up. "I do the same design every year. It's a witch."

"I can tell. I never knew you had such an artistic streak, Mrs. Nelson."

She flushes with obvious pride. "You charmer, you."

I give her a mock salute. "All part of the service, ma'am."

She looks between Keira and me before she leans in toward me. Of course, she's almost half my height, so I've got to lean right down to meet her.

"What's going on with you and Ms. Johnson over here? Word on the street is you're giving her nephew some hockey lessons."

"Benny's a great kid," I reply, evading her real question. "He's got a lot of potential. I'm just trying to give him a head start."

"Be that as it may, people are wondering why you've singled Benny out and not some other children. Ice hockey has become very popular in this town since you made it into the National League, you know. Every Tom, Dick, and Harry wants to be the next Dan Roberts. Which got me thinking that perhaps you had some hidden agenda, if you know what I mean." She raises her brows at me in question.

So, the townsfolk are talking about me and Keira. They're

more on the money than I care to admit, but without having even had a conversation about how I feel with the woman in question, I'm not exactly going to spill the beans for Mrs. Nelson.

"I think I'll just have to leave you guessing, Mrs. Nelson, because right now I'm here to carve a pumpkin."

"You are? Oh, goodie." She claps her hands together in delight. "Perhaps we could auction off your work of art? Raise some more money for the kiddies?"

I think the last time I carved a pumpkin, right here at this fall festival, it was an unmitigated disaster, the creative gene some members of my family seemed to have inherited clearly passing me by without so much as a glance my way.

"Let's just see how it works out first, shall we?" I straighten up just as she grabs my sleeve and says urgently, "You be sure to treat our Keira right. She's very important to us, here in Maple Falls, you know. No funny business. No messing her around. Got it?"

If only she knew.

"Got it," I reply with a smile.

A few moments later, I've talked Keira into carving, and sitting side by side, we work on our respective pumpkins with people dropping by to say hello to both of us. More than one comment is made about how it's like old times seeing Dan and Keira together, to which I simply smile and nod, throwing furtive glances Keira's way and catching her smiling.

Hope is beginning to build a sandcastle in my heart by now.

Keira eyes my creation. "What's yours meant to be?"

"Once I saw a pumpkin carved as a jack-o'-lantern with a part of the pumpkin hanging out of its mouth as though it were a tongue."

"Where's the tongue?"

I pick up a piece of pumpkin I carved out already and hold it up. "One tongue."

"That's a new one," she comments.

I eye her pumpkin. It's fair to say in a carving competition she would win hands down. She's carved an owl into the skin, complete with eyes, and has begun carving what looks like a tree. "Creative, but then you were always better at everything than me."

"With one notable exception."

"You mean dancing?" I tease.

Keira was so good at pretty much everything at school, with a perfect grade average and involvement in a bunch of extracurriculars, like the school paper. Physical stuff was less her thing, right down to dancing.

"I can dance," she replies indignantly.

My lips quirk. "Of course you can."

She shoots me a look, although I know it's in good humor. "At least my dancing is better than your singing. Need I remind you?"

I hold my hands up in the surrender sign. "I was never going to be a singer."

"And I was never going to be a dancer."

"I guess that makes us even."

"I guess it does, Dan Roberts."

"I like this," I murmur.

"Carving pumpkins?"

I nudge her with my elbow. "Yeah. That's what I mean," I joke, and we share a smile.

We may be surrounded by pumpkin carvers and festival goers and busy bodies like Mrs. Nelson telling me what to do, but I don't care. I want Keira to know how I feel.

It's now or never.

But then a little voice inside my head asks, what if she only wants to be friends? What if I've misread this whole situation? What if she's happy to keep what we had in the past? Because if that's how she responds, if that's what she truly wants, then the torch of hope I've been carrying with me all these years, the torch that has grown into a bonfire, will be extinguished forever.

I glance at this beautiful woman at my side, mouth twisted as she concentrates hard on her carving.

All my hopes could be extinguished by her in one short sentence.

I'm not ready for that to happen. Not now. Not ever.

So, instead I finish up my pumpkin and enjoy the moment with her, sitting side by side with the woman I love, still holding out the hope that she does still love me, just as I still love her.

CHAPTER 10
KEIRA

I PEER over the top of my book, not wanting Dan to know I'm watching him. He's teaching Benny how to move on the ice as he nudges the puck with his stick, giving him encouragement and pointers. Every time I watch them together, my heart fills to the brim. I can't help it. The man who once meant so much to me—the man, I admit, who still means so much to me—helping one of my other favorite humans to realize a goal? Well, it can't but tug at my heartstrings like an eager dog on its leash.

As I watch Dan congratulate Benny after he hits the puck into the goal, I know I shouldn't, but I can't help imagining that Dan help but feel like a teenager next to her grown-up put togetherness.

"Hey, stranger. How are you?" I ask as we greet one another with a quick hug.

"Sorry, Kiki. I've been super busy," she complains as she takes a seat next to me. "My client isn't exactly easy."

"Cooper Montgomery?" I ask as I eye the bulky Travis Kelce—minus the smile—lookalike guy on the ice. "What are you talking about? He looks like a total comedian to me, B."

She lets out a laugh. "You can tell I've got my work cut out, right?"

"Oh, yeah."

She focuses on the rink, and I know she's watching Dan and Benny. "Is that Dan Roberts out there with a kid?"

"Sure is. He's teaching hockey to my nephew, Benny."

Her eyes widen as she turns to me. "Is he, now?"

"I didn't ask or anything like that. He offered and Benny so wants to be a hockey pro … so, you know," I reply hastily, trying not to allow the heat that's rapidly climbing my neck to bloom in my cheeks. I just know it's a mission doomed to abject failure.

"And why would he go doing a thing like that, I wonder," Blair says, tapping her chin as though she's deep in thought.

She's *such* an actress.

"As I said, Benny wants to be a hockey pro someday, just like Dan. He's being kind, I guess."

"Uh-huh." Her eyes are still on me, and I can't keep up the ruse.

"Look, I'm trying not to read anything into it because what will that do? It'll only get my hopes up and then I'll come crashing back to Earth when Dan leaves town again. I'm not going to put myself through that, B. Not again."

"Have you ever thought that maybe Dan's teaching your nephew so he can get close to you?"

I chew on my lip, a knot forming in my belly. "It had

occurred to me. He told me his number for the Ice Breakers is my birthday."

Her eyes widen. "Girl, if that's not a sign the guy wants to be with you, I don't know what is."

I chew on my lip. "He could just be being sentimental?"

She rolls her eyes. "Sure. NHL stars are such a sentimental bunch. What would be so terrible about exploring how he feels about you? You could just tell him how you feel and see what he says."

"Are you serious?" I splutter, my eyes at risk of popping out of my head they're so wide. "You want me to go up to him and say, 'Hey, Dan, you know how we broke up a lifetime ago and you're this big, famous NHL star these days, living in Chicago, and I still live in a small town in the middle of nowhere? Well, I wondered if you might want to, you know, get back together.'" I blanch at the mere idea. "I would rather volunteer to play goalie for the Ice Breakers."

She returns her attention to Benny and Dan. They're skating side by side, following a puck toward the goal. Dan's patience is obvious as Benny shoots for a goal and misses by a good eight feet.

"I don't know about you, but I don't see any of the other hockey pros teaching kids to play in their free time."

"I'm trying not to read too much into it," I say again.

"But?" she leads.

"But you're right. Dan's the only one teaching a Maple Falls kid, even though he's busy with practices and media things, not to mention the games starting up soon."

Her grin stretches from ear to ear. "Open those pretty blue eyes of yours. Dan Roberts wants you back. I would stake my reputation on it."

Knowing how seriously my career-oriented friend takes her livelihood, that's a bold statement.

She presses her hand to my forearm. "I know you're scared. I get that. But he's giving your nephew free lessons, turning up at your house, giving you his jersey, choosing your birthday as his number. The guy has feelings for you."

I worry my lip some more. "Maybe."

She shakes her head at me. "Tell him how you feel. What's the worst that can happen?"

I watch as he skates over to the edge of the rink, trailed by Benny, signaling the end of the lesson.

I know what the worst is that could happen. I could put myself out there, really out there, and he could reject me, leaving me alone again, here in Maple Falls.

CHAPTER 11
DAN

PRACTICE IS IN FULL SWING, and the sound of skates cutting the ice fills the rink. I line up for a face-off against Cooper, who's been his usual bad-tempered self all morning. He grunts as he sets his stance. "Ready to lose, Roberts?"

I smirk. "In your dreams, man."

The puck drops, and I win the face-off cleanly, sending it back to Ted on defense. My wrist twinges, but nothing more. Ted controls the puck smoothly and passes to Noah, who's already moving up the ice. I skate hard, keeping an eye on the play.

We're jelling well on the ice as a team, and I've got high

hopes will make a clean sweep of our matches. We're up against the Canadian Lumberjacks in all five matches, my old Blizzard's rival. Winning against the Jacks would be so sweet.

Coach blows the whistle, calling for a transition drill. We break into our lines, moving seamlessly from defense to offense.

Dawson is in net, focused and intense, just like he was back in our college days. Ted passes to me as I cross the blue line, and I quickly dish it to Cooper on the right wing. Despite his perpetually bad mood, Cooper's got hands like magic, and he snaps a shot that Dawson deflects with a quick glove save.

"Nice try, Coop!" I shout, circling back.

Coach's voice echoes through the rink, barking orders. "Keep it tight! Move the puck faster!"

We're in the middle of a play when Nate, our cocky left winger, decides to pull something risky. He's skating down the ice with a speed that borders on reckless, the puck glued to his stick. I can see that look in his eyes—he's up to something.

Nate charges toward the goal, defenders closing in on him from both sides. Instead of passing to an open teammate, he pulls a slick between-the-legs move, faking out both defensemen. Everyone seems to hold their breath as he then flips the puck up and over Dawson's shoulder, a move straight out of a highlight reel. Dawson barely has time to react before the puck hits the back of the net.

Nate skates away, grinning like a kid on Christmas morning. "Told you I got this!" he shouts, pumping his fist in the air.

Coach Strickland is not amused. He skates over, eyes blazing. "Nate, that was risky as heck! You pull something like that in a game, and it better work every time."

Nate just shrugs, still smiling. "Relax, Coach. If you got it, flaunt it, right?"

I can't help but smirk at his brash cockiness. But that's Nate for you: recklessly talented and as cocky as they come. At least he backs it up with skill. The team might grumble, but deep down, we all know he brings a spark that keeps us on our toes.

Coach switches things up, calling for power play practice. I take my spot at center, with Cooper and Noah on my wings.

"How's the injury?" Noah asks.

"Only giving me a little trouble," I reply.

Ted and Noah set up on the blue line, ready to feed us the puck. Scotty told us he wants quick puck movement, and we start cycling it around, looking for openings.

I see an opportunity and pass to Cooper, who hesitates, then fires a shot. This time, Dawson's prowess in the goal pays off, and he defends it.

"Better luck next time, Coop," he calls out.

We keep pushing, the practice intense but productive. Scotty keeps us on our toes, shouting instructions, and by the end, we're all ready for some kick back time—and my wrist for some rest. It's held up well today, but I don't want to push it. Getting another injury could see me out of the Ice Breakers, and that's the last thing I want.

After we've showered and changed, I walk with Dawson to our respective cars.

"That Nate," Dawson says with a shake of his head. "I thought Coach was going to pop a blood vessel at his antics."

"He's young and got a lot to prove. We were all a little like that at one time."

Throwing his gear in his trunk, he leans against his car, crossing his arms against the cold. "What's with you and your ex?"

I arrange my features carefully. "What do you mean?"

"Emmy said something about how people are talking about you guys."

I raise my brows in deflection. "My *sister* said that to you, huh?"

Dawson grins at me. "Yeah, we've been hanging out a little. She's cool."

"She is. She's the best." I narrow my eyes at my friend.

"Is now when you give me your 'be careful with my sister' speech? 'Cause you don't need to do that. I know she's special."

I pinch my lips together. "She is."

"But don't think I didn't notice that you totally avoided answering my question, man. You and your ex. Are you two hooking up? What's the deal?"

"We're not hooking up. I would never do that to Kiki. She's too—" I search for the right word to use.

Dawson raises his chin as he watches me, a knowing look on his face. "Oh. Right. It's like that."

"Like what exactly? I haven't said a word."

"You're in love with the girl," he says simply with a shrug, taking me by surprise.

Of course I'm in love with Keira. I've never *not* been in love with her. I've carried her in my heart since the day we met, my constant companion, my *everything*.

"I don't see you denying it."

I look him directly in the eye. "You're right, I'm not denying it."

"So? What are you gonna do about it, man?" Dawson prompts.

I clench my jaw. I've been so busy walking on eggshells around her, searching for any sign that she feels something for me still after all these years. Waiting. Hoping.

"I'm going to show her just how much she means to me," I say.

Forget waiting and wondering, hoping and praying. I need to act. I need to show her what she means to me.

I know what I want to do. What I *need* to do, and I need to do it right now.

Determined, I open the door to my SUV and get inside, slamming the door behind me. As I turn the ignition, Dawson knocks on the window.

I press the button to lower it.

"What the heck? You can't just leave in the middle of a conversation," he says on a laugh.

"I've made my mind up. I'm going to tell Kiki how I feel."

He raises his brows. "That you love her?"

I nod, a smile busting out on my face. "That I love her."

Dawson raises his hands in the air, stepping back from my car. "Far be it for me to stand in the way of true love."

True love.

"As cheesy as this sounds, man—go get your girl."

And that's exactly what I intend to do.

CHAPTER 12
KEIRA

"WHY ARE YOU SUDDENLY PLAYING MATCHMAKER?" I ask Clara as we sit at the kitchen table to eat our dinner. I'd actually cooked tonight—a rare occurrence in this household. I view myself more as an assembler of meals rather than a cook per se, other than my famous pumpkin pie, of course, which is a total labor of love. The fact that I roasted a chicken, complete with potatoes, pumpkin, and broccoli is no small feat.

"What's a matchmaker?" Benny asks. "Oh, I know. It's like that box of matches above the fireplace. Can you make those,

Mommy?"

"That's not what it is," Hannah declares confidently, so much wiser at her eight years of age.

"What is it then, sweetie?" Clara asks her, no doubt stalling for time.

"It's when someone can see that two people love each other and so they put them together so they will live happily ever after." Hannah smiles at us all, satisfied with her surprisingly accurate and mature definition.

"Wow, sweetie. You've got that spot on," Clara says as she lovingly smooths down her daughter's hair. "I've got a couple of smart kids. Don't I, Aunt Kiki?"

"You sure do," I reply with a smile. "But that doesn't answer my question." I take a bite of roasted potato. It's surprisingly good, considering I cooked it. Not as good as Mom's, of course, but nothing I make is.

"Can't you allow your poor sister a little entertainment from her sick bed?" Clara replies, pulling out the CFS card.

I shake my head. "Oh, no. You can't pull the sick card on me, sis. You're definitely matchmaking us."

"Who? Who is mommy matchmaking you with? Who do you love?" Hannah demands.

I give Clara a look. "Your mom knows."

"Who, Mommy?" Hannah asks.

"Just the perfect man for your aunt. They used to date in high school, and they were the cutest couple back then, and by the looks of things, at least one of them wants to be a cute couple once more, if a certain number on a jersey is anything to go by."

Hannah looks at her mom blankly.

"Maybe we should take this conversation offline?" I suggest, and thankfully Clara agrees, and she drops the topic until it's just her and me in the kitchen, cleaning up after dinner.

"And?" she leads.

"And what?"

"You know exactly what. You and Dan."

I press my lips together as I wipe a tea towel across a cleaned dinner plate. "There is no me and Dan."

"I know there isn't right now, but there should be. Not only is he teaching Benny how to play hockey, but he came by here to give you his jersey *with your birthdate on it*. How much more obvious does he have to get?"

"He gave all of us his jersey."

"Only because he wants you to wear it."

"I would be a fool to pin my hopes on something like that. Most of the town will be wearing Dan's jersey at the games. He's the small-town guy made good in the NHL, after all. 'Dan the Man.'"

She gives me a satisfied smile, so I busy myself with drying off another dinner plate. "You do realize you've just given away how you feel about the guy."

Busted.

I turn to face her. "How I feel about him is completely irrelevant. He's only here in town for six weeks, and then he'll be gone."

"And you can continue pining for him from a distance?"

"I don't want to put myself on the line for someone who left for bigger and brighter things the first time 'round. I'm the girl he left behind, remember? I don't want to feel like that again when he leaves in a few weeks. So, really, how I feel about him is completely irrelevant because it won't stop him leaving. *Again*."

She's still got that annoying, satisfied smile on her face, like she knows something that I don't know.

"What?" I ask in exasperation.

"Did you notice anything when you came home today?"

I pull my eyebrows together. "I don't know what you're talking about."

"Think about it. You pulled your car into the driveway as usual. Then you got out of your car and walked up the steps to come through the front door."

"Where are you going with this? I don't think I need a blow-by-blow of how I entered the house, riveting as it is."

She throws her hand on her hips. "Are you purposely not getting this?"

"What's there to get?"

"The step. It was broken this morning when you left, and now ..."

I narrow my eyes at her. "What has the broken step got to do with Dan?"

"It seems I'm going to have to spell this out to you. Dan came over this afternoon when you were out."

My heart rate jumps at the thought of Dan coming to my house again. "He did?"

Clara nods. "He brought a hammer and nails."

"Why would he bring—" My mind finally catches up on what Clara is telling me. "Dan fixed the broken step?" I ask, my voice coming out all breathy.

Her knowing smile morphs into a broad grin. "He fixed the step."

Clara looks out the kitchen window, and I hear the rumble of an engine. "Oh, and one other thing, sis. He's coming back to take you out, right about now."

"Wait, what?!" I squeal, my pulse banging against my ribs like a caged animal trying to escape. Dan fixed the step? And now he's here to take me out?

"Did I not tell you?" Clara asks, her face bright.

"I might have remembered that if you had!" I reply, clutching a tea towel and plate in my hands. "Is it a date? As in a proper date? It's a date, isn't it? Clara?"

My sister is now beaming like the Cheshire cat. "It's a date." She places a hand on my shoulder. "Be careful. Okay, Keeks?"

"Be careful? Why?" I ask, confused, as I peer out the window at Dan, closing the door of his SUV and making his way toward the entrance to the house.

Dan. Here. Taking me on a date.

I might pass out.

"Because, Kiki, you might just get everything you ever wanted."

I open my mouth to reply when there's a knock at the door and I swear my heart almost gives out with the knowledge that Dan is standing on my doorstep—the fixed doorstep, thanks to him—waiting for me.

"Well? Are you going to answer the door?" Clara asks when I don't move.

"The door. Right." On shaking legs, I leave the kitchen, still clutching onto my tea towel and dinner plate as though they're my safety blanket. I can see Dan's bulk and his broad shoulders through the glass of the front door, and I suck in a deep breath, my hand on the doorknob before I turn it and pull the door open.

"Hey," I murmur as I take him in. He's wearing a grey sweater with a zip at the neck, open to show a white T-shirt underneath, which he's paired with some dark dress pants and sneakers. He looks ridiculously handsome and oh-so hot and looking at him I finally understand the expression "he took my breath away." Because that's exactly what happens to me right now.

"Hi, Kiki," he replies, looking nervous.

Dan Roberts is standing on my doorstep, looking nervous.

I feel like I'm in some kind of weird parallel universe.

"You fixed the step."

His lips quirk into a soft smile. "I didn't want you to fall and hurt yourself."

Oh, my.

"That's so kind of you. Thank you."

"There's no need to thank me," he says quietly. "I did it because I wanted to."

My breath is coming out ragged, and I'm resisting the urge to throw myself into his arms and tell him I love him right here and now. But I resist. When it comes to Dan, I've guarded my heart for so very long, it's become a habit.

No matter how much I want to be with him.

"I'm going to thank you all the same," I reply.

"In that case, you're welcome. I was hoping to take you out tonight, if you're free?"

I smile as a mélange of nerves, excitement, and anticipation swirl around me. "I'd like that."

Footsteps thunder down the hallway, and an excited Benny almost bowls me over as he comes to a crashing halt, wrapping his arms around my waist.

He peers up at Dan. "Are you here to give me a lesson?" he asks hopefully.

Dan smiles down at him. "Sorry, buddy. Not tonight. Tonight, I'm taking your aunt out."

Benny looks from Dan to me and back again. "Is that because of the matchmaking? And I don't mean the ones above the fireplace. I mean the love matches."

I stifle an embarrassed giggle as Dan gives me a questioning look. "There was talk of matchmaking at the dinner table tonight," I explain.

"Got it," Dan replies. "Is it okay if I hang out with your aunt tonight and we have our lesson after the first game?"

"Okay, I guess," Benny replies, clearly expecting that when Dan is around, a lesson is on offer.

"I'll go get my coat," I tell him. "Why don't you come in?"

"I'll check in on that step while I wait."

I grin. "You do that." I rush down the hall and give Clara a hug, my eyes filling with tears. "You're the best," I tell her.

"You know it. Now go. Have a great night."

I beam at her, the thought of being out on a date with Dan filling my body with spikes of electricity, my heart beating right out of my chest.

I throw on my jacket and check my appearance in the

hallway mirror. Not exactly dressed for a date, but I get the feeling Dan won't care about something like that.

A short and nervous drive later and he pulls into a parking space outside Falling for Books. All the stores on Main Street are dark with "closed" signs hanging in their windows, and I wonder why he's brought me here.

"Are we meeting Emmy?" I ask as Dan unhooks his seatbelt.

"Not exactly," is his elusive reply. He climbs out of the car, and I follow suit, standing on the sidewalk of the deserted Main Street.

To my surprise he pulls out a key and unlocks the front door of his sister's bookstore. "After you," he says, holding the door open, and confused, I step inside the darkened store.

"Come with me." Dan takes my hand in his, the unexpected feel of skin against skin sending a delicious jolt through me, rendering my bones so they feel like liquid honey.

Wow. If I respond like this to a simple touch of his hand, how will I ever cope if he actually kisses me?

He leads me to the back of the store to the coffee shop, with the soft glow of lamps and the comforting presence of books surrounding us. One of the tables has been moved closer to the bookshelves, covered in a crisp white tablecloth, with a single unlit candle and a cardboard box labeled *Maple Grounds* sitting at the center. There are fairy lights hanging from the ceiling that I know weren't there before, and as he clicks the light switch, they're like little stars glowing around us.

"You did this?" I ask.

"I wanted to do something special for you, and I know how much books mean to you. The fact my sister runs this place made it a whole lot easier to manage."

"Emmy's the best."

"She is," he agrees.

I look around in wonder. Dan arranged all this with his sister … for me. If my brain had successfully squashed my greatest desire earlier this evening, it completely fails to have any impact whatsoever now. Hope is pumping through my very veins, telling me I could be about to get everything I've ever wanted, just as Clara said.

"Why don't you take a seat?" Dan asks as he pulls out one of the chairs from the table.

"All right." I take a seat and watch as he lights the candle. It casts a soft glow over the table, amping up the romance that already feels through the roof.

"Would you like a drink? I got Emmy to teach me how to make your favorite coffee. Mocha, right?"

"You learned how to use the coffee machine for me?" I ask in astonishment. Astonishment and pure, unadulterated delight, that is.

He grins. "Is that so hard to believe?"

"It's ... no, it's not. You always were kind."

Kind and thoughtful and everything wonderful.

He holds my gaze, and all my nerves evaporate like steam into the atmosphere. Sure, I may have been secretly wishing he was mine all these years, but there's nothing to be nervous about anymore.

This is Dan. I know him. I love him. There's nothing more to know.

"How about that coffee?" he asks.

"I'd love a mocha. Thank you."

"One mocha coming up," he says as he makes his way around the counter.

I sit and watch him wield the machine, the occasional huff leaving his lips, his brows pulled together. He looks totally adorable, this huge sports pro working the machine, and I smile as I watch him.

"You sure you don't need any help?" I ask.

"Nope," he replies. "You're my guest. I've got this."

"Guests can help out, you know. I was a part-time barista at a Seattle coffeehouse during college."

"I heard about that," he says before he grinds the beans.

"You did?"

"Ask around and you find out pretty quick that folks around here have a grand total of zero secrets."

I've managed to keep my feelings about you *secret from the folks in Maple Falls,* I think as he tamps down the coffee into the bulb as though he's some kind of coffee expert.

But then Clara guessed it. And although Blair's not from Maple Falls, she's in town right now and she knows. And so does Ellie.

Hmm. Okay, so maybe I haven't kept my feelings for Dan all *that* secret.

But right now, as I watch the man I've never gotten over, work the machine to make me my favorite coffee, that does not matter at all.

"You've been asking around about me?" I ask, embarrassed—but elated.

The skin around his eyes crinkles as his lips tilt in a smile. "Only Emmy and Troy and Kelly and a few others."

I'm grinning so hard my face feels like it might crack. "I see."

"I realized my Keira Johnson file was missing some vital details. It needed an update."

"Details like I'm not married with kids?"

"Exactly." His gaze lingers on mine for a beat before he seems to remember he's in the middle of making coffee. "Time for the milk." He furrows his brow in the most adorable way once more as he concentrates hard on steaming the milk, the familiar hissing and gurgling sounds filling the air.

Once done, he brings the coffee over to the table and places it carefully in front of me. "One mocha for my guest. Take a sip."

"Thank you," I reply. I lift the mug to my lips to taste it. "It's good."

He sits down opposite me at the little table. "Don't sound so surprised."

"I admit I am surprised. You're a pro hockey player, not a barista."

He shrugs. "You know me. When I want something, I stop at nothing until I get it."

The atmosphere between us shifts, his words hanging in the air. Am I the something he wants? Will he stop at nothing to get me?

Popping the box on the table open, he says, "I know how much you like the baked goods from Maple Grounds. You always had a sweet tooth."

He offers me the box and I spy six cinnamon rolls, each looking utterly delicious. My mouth begins to water.

"This is so sweet of you." I pick up one of the rolls. "How did you know I liked these so much?"

"You were clutching onto one when I saw you in the bleachers."

I wince with embarrassment. "That was unbelievable. I can't believe I did that."

He smiles. "I thought it was cute."

I offer him a shy look. "It was the first time we'd seen one another since we broke up all those years ago. It wasn't exactly my finest moment."

"Actually, I saw you a couple times on my visits home."

"You did?"

"Yup. Once at the diner, just down the road from here. You were in a back booth. I was plucking up the courage to come over to talk to you, but I got distracted by some people wanting selfies. When I looked back, you were gone."

Do I tell him I ran away? Heck, he caught me hiding in the bleachers. On the embarrassment scale, running away from him scores maybe a five out of ten, not the ten out of ten I scored for hiding.

"I snuck out the back," I admit.

His brows ping up. "You did? Why?"

"Because you looked so happy and you had this big, glamorous career that came with fame and everything else, and here I was still living in our small town, not exactly living my best life."

"You see, that's where you're wrong. I think you are leading your best life. You're so enmeshed in this place, Kiki. You know everyone, they know and respect you, you're part of the fabric of the community. Do you know how much I envy that?"

If only I hadn't taken a sip of my coffee at that very moment, I might not have sprayed it all over the white tablecloth. "Oops," I say as I dab at the splatters with the sleeve of my jacket.

"Forget about it," Dan says, placing his hand over mine.

I look up into his eyes and feel a rush of warmth and peace. His gaze is steady, soft, and filled with an unspoken promise that somehow manages to reach deep into my soul.

With my chest tight, I ask, "Dan, what are we doing?"

His lips quirk. "Drinking coffee and eating cinnamon rolls, by the look of things."

I can't help but return his smile. "I think you know what I mean."

"I do." He takes a breath, lowering his eyes to our entwined hands before raising them back to mine. "I brought you here tonight because I know how much you love to read. This place is special to you, and I wanted to show you it's one of the things I love about you."

Love.

His mention of that four-letter word has my breath hitching in my throat.

"I know it's been a long time since we've been together. A lifetime. But I wanted you to know that I've never forgotten about you. I've always held you here with me." He places his hand over his chest. "The truth is, no one has ever compared to you, my kind, beautiful, smart Kiki."

My heart expands to twice its size and I could not stop the grin from claiming my face for all the trees in Washington state.

"I thought you'd moved on. I was sure of it. It's been so long."

"I know. Everyone told me I would find other loves, that you were just my first."

"They told me that, too."

"Kiki, my love, you're it for me, but I've been too focused on my career, too blinded, too stupid to let you know. And right now, I'm totally putting myself out there, hoping against all odds that somehow you feel the same way about me."

Tears spring to my eyes, my body shaking, barely believing the words that are leaving his mouth. This is what I've always wanted. Dan still in love with me. Dan wants to be with me.

"No one has ever compared to you, either," I reply, my voice trembling.

In one swift move he rises from his chair and is beside me, pulling me to my feet. He holds me close against his muscular body, his large arms enveloping me.

I look up into his eyes moments before his lips come crashing against mine, holding me tight. I'm lost in him, the way it feels to be wrapped up by this big, strong man I've never been able to forget, all my fears and anxieties whisked away as our kiss deepens. He's showing me how much he loves me. How much he wants me. And I can barely believe this is happening after wanting it for so, so long.

After we come up for air, he looks down at me, grinning. "I love you, Keira Johnson. With all my heart. I love you."

"I love you too, Dan."

"Why did we leave this so long?" he asks on a light laugh.

"I guess we were just a couple of idiots."

He lifts me up and I wrap my legs around his waist as he kisses me again. "You know I'm never letting you go ever again, right?"

I let out a giddy laugh. "You'd better not."

"I promise," he whispers, kissing me once more, and I melt into him, my Dan once more, the man I love.

CHAPTER 13
DAN

IT'S the night of the Ice Breakers' first game, and the atmosphere in the arena is electric. Having visited with my parents, Mimi, and Emmy yesterday, I know that the whole town is turning out tonight—and practically all of them are wearing my jersey.

But there's only one person I want to see wearing my jersey. Keira.

Since we confessed our feelings for one another that night at Emmy's bookshop, we've spent as much time together as our schedules will allow—which isn't nearly as much as I would like. I've got practices, PT sessions, and all the publicity stuff we've got to do for the team and games, as well as gym workouts and spending time with my family. For her part, Keira has her job, running around after her niece and nephew, and caring for her sister.

So, yeah. Not a lot of time.

But what time we have spent together has been incredible. Being with Keira is just as I had always imagined it. We get each other. We click. And it's so much more than simply because we grew up together and dated in high school. We're soulmates, pure and simple. And it feels amazing to finally be with her after all this time.

"How's the wrist?" Scotty asks.

I hold up my gloved left hand. "Like new."

"You sure? The last thing we want is you getting hurt out there. This is only the first game. We need you leading the team for the whole series."

"I got the all-clear from the PT to play, Coach, and I'm doing good."

He slaps me on the back. "Good luck out there."

"Thanks."

My teammates and I wait in the tunnel, ready to head out onto the ice when our names are announced. The excitement is palpable. Sure, each player here plays professionally for other teams, some in the NHL, some in the lower leagues, and this series is an unpaid gig which we're doing for kids in need. We might be the team Troy Hart brought together, but tonight, we're the Ice Breakers, a real team. And we're ready to take on our opponent for the first time, the Canadian Lumberjacks.

The familiar and rousing beat of our team song begins to play, and the crowd erupts into excited cheers and applause.

Dawson flashes me a grin. "Remind you of our college days?" he shouts over the noise.

"I don't remember 'Ice Ice Baby' playing back then," I joke as Vanilla Ice tells us to kick it. "And nor do I remember a dancing otter as our mascot."

He laughs. "Yeah, what's with that? But you know I meant you and me, on a team together. I like it."

I grin back at him. "Yeah. Lots of memories, man. Good memories."

The emcee announces the first players, and we move up closer to the ice as each guy skates out to uproarious cheers.

"Let's get out there and smash it," Dawson says over the noise.

I raise my gloved hand and fist bump his. "You got it."

"Introducing Ted 'the Bear' Powell, defenseman!" the emcee announces and Ted flashes us a grin before he skates out onto the rink to cheers.

"Join me in giving a huge Maple Falls welcome to Dawson Hayes, goalie!" the emcee announces, and I watch as Dawson skates out ahead of me.

Finally, it's my turn. Being the homegrown hero and the captain, Coach made me go last, knowing I'll get the biggest reaction from the crowd.

"And finally, tonight, the center for the Chicago Blizzard, a man who needs no introduction, Ice Breakers captain and hometown hero, Dan Roberts, better known as 'Dan the Man'!"

I step onto the ice to the biggest cheer of the night and look around at a sea of number 29 jerseys, the crowd cheering and screaming my nickname, and banners with "Dan the Man!" "Roberts on Ice, Victory in Sight!" and "Roberts Rules the Ice!" I spot a few supporting the team, "Ice Breakers Freeze the Opposition!" and "Breaking the Ice with the Ice Breakers!" which makes me feel better—it's not all about me, after all. We're a team, and every cog in the wheel matters.

I wave at the crowd to more cheers, the buzz electric.

Man! This never gets old. Skating out onto the ice in front of a huge crowd alongside my teammates, knowing we've got one another's backs, vying for the win.

Only this time, the feeling is even better because this time, I've got the woman I love out there in the bleachers—the very bleachers she hid beneath only a few short weeks ago—cheering me on, wearing my jersey. I haven't had that feeling since I played in high school, and it feels fantastic.

I know exactly where she's sitting and I look up to the section, searching for Keira. My eyes land on her in a sea of number 29 jerseys. She's grinning and waving at me, her gorgeous blonde hair falling in soft waves over her shoulders, the look on her beautiful face filling me with love.

And then the puck drops, and the game is on. I'm at center, eyes locked on McNeil, the cocky Lumberjacks' star player. He's got control, weaving through our defense like a snake, just as he has in countless games I've played against him in the League.

But then Nate intercepts McNeil's pass with a deft flick of his stick. The crowd roars as he bolts down the ice, threading through defenders like they're standing still. He eyes Cooper and passes the puck with pinpoint accuracy as I get into position, hoping for my own shot at a goal. With a quick glance, Cooper sends the puck my way, gliding smoothly, and I catch it with my stick. Time slows as I line up my shot, laser-focused. I can almost see the goalie's eyes widen, and I spot my opening.

I strike.

It's as though the entire arena is holding its collective breath as the puck sails past the goalie's outstretched glove, slamming into the back of the net with a satisfying *whack!* The red light flashes. It's a goal!

The crowd erupts and instinctively, I look up at Keira. She's on her feet, cheering for me along with Benny and Hannah, who are bouncing up and down as though they're on a trampoline.

Cooper skates over, grinning, and we exchange a triumphant fist bump. Nate joins us, and we celebrate together. This is what we live for—only I've got something even more important to live for now, and before my brain even catches up with what I'm doing, I've skated over to the plexiglass in front of Keira where I blow her a kiss.

All heads turn to look at who I'm aiming for, and Keira's flushing face tells them exactly what they want to know.

She mock glares at me, and I shrug, grinning.

The cat is well and truly out of the bag now, and I could not be happier.

I return to my position, and we launch back into the game. With every slice of my skates, with every hit of the puck, with every slam against the plexiglass, my heart beats for Keira.

The Lumberjacks manage to score a goal, and before we know it, we're in the final moments of the game, the score tied at 1-1. It's anyone's game now, but I hope it's ours. The Jacks' right wing, McNeil, gets a hold of the puck again. Defensemen Ted and Noah are on high alert, determined to protect the net. But McNeil is relentless, gliding down the ice, flanked by his teammates, Carter and Diaz, and I just know his eyes are locked on the prize.

Noah steps up to block McNeil's path, but with a slick maneuver, McNeil slips past both Noah and Ted as he passes the puck to Diaz with a swift flick. Diaz rockets forward, drawing Ted out of position. And that's when it happens. McNeil seizes the moment, darting into the opening and Dawson braces for impact. I can almost feel it before it happens, the puck hitting the back of the net. As McNeil winds up and slaps the puck, it sails past Dawson's knee and slams into its target.

The red light flashes, and we know, with only seconds on the clock, we've lost. Lumberjacks' supporters erupt in cheers, and our supporters groan. After a valiant attempt by the guys to score another goal, the final buzzer sounds, and the game ends in a crushing 2-1 defeat. It's not the way we—or the town—wanted this to go, but we can still hold our heads high, knowing that our newly formed team held the mighty Canadian Lumberjacks back from a much larger defeat.

As McNeil and his teammates celebrate, I take a deep breath and skate to the center, raising my stick to acknowledge the people of Maple Falls who've turned out in force to support us.

Despite the loss, their cheers and applause ring out, with cries of "We still love you, Dan the Man!" and "Ice Breakers rule!" from the crowd.

Once more, I find Keira's face in the crowd. She shrugs and smiles, as if to say you win some, you lose some, and I smile back at her.

We might have lost the game, but I've won back the person who's been missing from my world for what feels like a lifetime.

As is the custom, we line up to shake hands with the opposing team, showing our respect for the game. Afterward, we gather in a tight huddle, Coach giving us a few words of encouragement.

"Tough night, guys, and not the way I bet you wanted your first game to go, but you did yourselves proud," Coach says. "We've got a few things to work on at practice, but I'll give you the rest of the night off."

There are groans from my teammates, but I know as well as the next guy that after a defeat, you've got no choice but to pick yourselves up, regroup, and fix what failed in the game. Success in professional sport is as much of a mind game as it is a physical one, and a positive attitude and strong desire to win will get you places. This might not be the League, and we might not have played together as a team before, but we're all competitive guys with a need to win. We'll come back, better than before.

"Wrist okay out there?" Coach asks me, and it occurs to me I didn't once give it thought during the game.

"It's great, Coach," I reply.

"Good man."

We do a final skate around the rink, applauding the crowd before we head off the ice and out into the locker rooms.

I shower and change, ready to face the media—and the people of Maple Falls, as the Ice Breakers' team captain.

Just as I did when I was out on the ice, I find Keira in the crowd. She smiles at me, and warmth spreads through my chest.

We might have lost the game, but I've won the girl.

"A disappointing result for a first game," one of the journalists leads. "Do you think your team is up for the task?"

This isn't my first rodeo. I've had media training and plenty of experience. I know how to spin a response to work in my favor as well as the next guy. Troy told me he chose me as captain for a bunch of reasons, including the fact I'm good with the press. I know how to work with a group of guys on the ice, and I know how to answer difficult questions.

"We're a brand-new team. We've not played together before. I know that's no excuse, but we've got a bunch of super talented guys on the team. We will regroup and come back stronger than before. Every game is a new opportunity, and we intend to grab that opportunity and run with it."

I turn my attention from that particular journalist to a young, nervous looking guy in the front row.

"Why did you choose number 29 for the new team?" he asks.

"Someone very special to me is born on that date," I reply.

"Who?"

"Someone special," I repeat. I spot my mom and dad, standing next to Keira at the back of the room, and throw them a smile.

"You know something? My parents are one of the reasons I'm here today, and I don't just mean alive. They were instrumental in that, too, though." Laughter rolls through the room. "My parents supported me in my goal to make it to the NHL. They sacrificed a lot, and I'm honored that they're here with me tonight."

Heads swivel and my grinning dad gives a salute. Mom beams.

"Did you feel there were any specific turning points or key moments in the game?" another journalist asks, an older man with a comb over. I recognize him as Burt Hamilton, a journalist from back East.

"Like when the Lumberjacks scored that second goal?" I joke.

"Yeah, there were a few. We need to tighten up our defense, and we'll be working on that in practice."

"You were benched by the Blizzard for a wrist injury and got special dispensation to play for the Ice Breakers. That's not usually the way these things play out. How's the injury now?" Burt asks.

"I've had a lot of rest and rehab here in Washington. I'm cautiously optimistic I'm good."

An attractive female journalist calls out, "What's the most interesting or surprising thing a fan has done to try to get your attention romantically?"

I flick my gaze briefly to Keira's. "Pretending to look for a contact lens."

"Can you explain that?" the journalist asks.

"I can't. But it worked."

I know I'm being elusive. But seriously, what's my personal life got to do with the game? Don't get me wrong, there's always someone at these things who asks personal questions, and there's always much speculation about who we players are dating, so I guess I'm used to it. But it's not their business.

"Who were you blowing kisses at?" she asks.

"Someone special."

"A girl?"

"Maybe."

"You're not giving much away here, Mr. Roberts."

I simply smile at her.

She tries another angle. "Your name was linked with Christy Mahoney not that long ago," she continues, referring to a model I dated briefly last season. "Rumor has it she's coming to the next game. Is that for any romantic reason?"

"I had no idea Christy Mahoney was coming to the next game," I reply honestly. I haven't even spoken to her since we dated briefly last winter. "But it'll be good to see her."

"So, does that mean you're single? Your female fans are eager to know," she persists.

I press my lips together. "How about we keep the questions to ice hockey?" I say before I lift my chin at another journalist who asks me a more appropriately hockey-related question.

A couple questions later, Troy, Zach, Scotty, and Coach Strickland thank everyone for being here and we get up to leave. I have plans to see Keira, and I'm excited to get to her.

As I make my way down the hallway, a group of fans approaches me, holding out pens and my jersey. A lone figure steps away from the crowd, holding up a camera and her press pass.

"Hey Dan," she says with an easy grin. "Mind if I take a few quick pics for *Athletic Edge*?"

Hearing the name of the magazine, I remember why I know her. We met for a photoshoot a few months back when her magazine featured me in the run up for the charity games.

"Sure," I say, pausing. I pull my lips into a smile and I hear the camera clicking away. She's done in no time. "It's Willa, right?"

"It is," she beams, obviously pleased I remember. "I won't hold you up. I'll see you 'round."

"See you 'round," I echo.

She jogs away, and I turn my attention back to the small crowd gathered around me. "How are you all doing tonight?" I ask as I sign the shirts.

"It's a shame you lost," replies a woman in her early-twenties, by the looks of her.

"It was," I confirm because what else can I say?

"Me and my friends were rooting for you to win." She indicates a group of women, all wearing thin clothing that must have had them freezing in the ice-cold arena.

"I hope we'll do better for everyone next time," I reply with a breezy smile as more jerseys and other merch are thrust my way to sign. I sign a bunch before I say, "Have a great night."

As I smile at them in farewell and begin to move down the hallway, the woman I recognize as Lana, the one who wanted me to sign my jersey while she was wearing it at the Maple Fest, grabs my sleeve.

"We thought you might like to come back to our hotel room for a drink," she purrs as she toys with her hair. "You could bring your teammates, if you wanted to, especially that Nate Simpson. He's cute, though not as cute as you."

I look at the women. They're all dressed the same way as Lana, virtually the puck bunny uniform of form-fitting crop tops, tight pants, and—at least for a couple of them—bunny ears on top of their heads.

"Thanks for the offer, ladies, but I've got team stuff to do," I reply, using an excuse I've relied on in the past to extricate myself from situations. "You have a great night."

"Don't go!" several of them squeal, pawing at me.

"Yeah, Dan. Don't go," Lana purrs as she clasps my arm.

This is getting out of hand.

"Sorry, but I've gotta go," I say, deftly stepping out from their grasp and darting down the hall, aiming for the exit. Sometimes being 6'5" is an advantage off the ice as well as on.

Some guys love this kind of attention, and I admit, when I was a rookie, I could not believe how easy it was to attract females. All I had to do was play for the team and afterwards, there'd be a bunch of women waiting to meet me—and more.

But those days are long behind me, and all I want to do is get to Keira, to hold her in my arms, and forget about tonight's loss.

It's then that I see her, standing in front of me, looking crestfallen in my jersey, and I wonder how much she's just seen. However much it is, I'm sure she'll understand. It's not like I solicited the women's attention. She'll know they're only interested in me because I'm a pro hockey player. It's got nothing to do with the real me.

"Let's get out of here, okay?" I say as I place a hand on her elbow and lead her away from the mob of persistent women.

"Good idea," she replies, and we push through the exit and out into the cool fall night. Together, just the way I want us to be.

CHAPTER 14
KEIRA

I'M in a totally loved-up daze with Dan. There's no other way to put it.

Since that night in the bookstore when we confessed our feelings for one another—and made my *life*—we've seen each other as much as we can, which isn't nearly as often as either of us would like, what with his practices, games, and captain responsibilities, and my job, the kids, and Clara.

But when we're together, grabbing the small amount of free time we can get—it's like a dream. It's everything I never dared hope for. Everything I've wanted since that terrible day we broke up and Dan left town.

What can I say? Being with Dan is utterly perfect.

Well, not quite *perfect* perfect. That's not possible, and I know I can't expect everything to be totally amazing. That's unrealistic. And it's ninety-nine point five percent amazing. Really.

And that point five percent isn't something I'm planning on talking to Dan about. Nope. There's nothing I could do about it, anyway. It is what it is, as the saying goes.

But here's the thing. Back in high school, Dan was always the popular one of us. Not that I ever liked to use labels, but he was the jock to my nerd. Total extrovert; captain of the super-successful ice hockey team; people would greet him with high fives, slaps on the back, and handshakes wherever we went. Girls would flirt with him. He was a star, even back then. People adored him. He shone.

It was a lot. Now, don't get me wrong. I never begrudged him that attention. He's the kind of person who attracts others, the type of person who draws people into his orbit. Heck, I was one of those people. But back then I could cope with it. Almost. It was restricted to our high school and our small town in the middle of nowhere.

Now, it's a whole other ball game. Or puck game, more appropriately. It feels like it's the whole country wanting to congratulate him, to be with him, to wear his jersey. To flirt with him.

Of course I get it. He's a big deal around here. He's our hometown hero. Blair told me her client, Cooper Montgomery, was surprised there wasn't a statue of Dan in the town square, he's so adored. He might have been saying it tongue in cheek, but it speaks volumes. These days that adoration goes way beyond our town. Those women who mobbed him at the arena after the first game were definitely more than fan-girling over him. There was something of the predator about them, like Dan was their prey and they weren't going to stop until they had him in their clasp.

I saw it all.

I made out that it wasn't a big deal and that I could cope with the attention he received, even though I could never compete with girls like that back in high school, and Dan never made me feel as though I had to. But I've got eyes. I know I'm not like them. I don't have their confidence, their sex appeal, their *shininess*. I love living in my small town, knowing everyone, running the farmers' market, stopping to chat to the locals about their hip replacements or gardens or what happened on their favorite TV show last night. I love hanging out at Falling for Books, sipping on a mocha, diving into the world of books.

I guess I love the quiet, simple things—and Dan's world is anything but quiet and simple.

Along with the rest of the town, I went to the second game, cheering just as loudly as everyone else when each member of the team was announced to the team's theme song of "Ice Ice Baby," celebrating each goal they won, commiserating with the fans each time the Jacks smashed the puck into the net. I wore my Dan Roberts number 29 jersey along with the rest of the town, delighting when the final buzzer blared, the Ice Breakers victorious.

Dan celebrated by blowing me a kiss from the ice, and I blushed, knowing all eyes were on me, judging me as Dan's girl, just the way they did back in high school.

I know I should be okay with it all. Dan loves me, something he shows me every single day.

But it's one thing knowing something, and quite another to fully and wholeheartedly believe it.

"A penny for them?" Dan asks, and I look from the glass in my hand up into his soft and smiling eyes, the party celebrating the Ice Breakers narrow 4-3 win in full swing around us.

"It's just work. I've leased a stall to a small olive oil producer, and they haven't been paying their lease."

It's a bald-faced lie. In my defense, I'm not exactly going to say *I don't feel good enough for you and I can never compete with your life*, am I? Not here at the party, anyway.

Maybe not ever.

"Do you want my advice?" he asks as he pulls me to my feet.

"Sure thing."

"Forget about work, and dance with me." He grins before he pulls me against him, swaying to the music. He's warm, big, and firm, and as I wrap my arms around him, I tell myself not to sweat the small stuff. It's a point five percent doubt, which is a tiny fraction of a percent.

This man loves me, and I love him back.

That's all that matters.

"You know you really do look extra beautiful tonight, Kiki," he murmurs into my ear. It sends a shiver down my neck.

"Is it because I'm in your jersey?" I jest.

He swirls me around and dips me, grinning down at me. "That's exactly why."

I chortle. "Well, in that case you must think most of the people at this party are looking extra beautiful tonight."

"Ah, but you see, they're not you," is his reply.

"And what's so good about me?" I ask before I can stop myself. I sound like I'm fishing for a compliment.

He pulls me against him, holding me close. "Didn't some famous person say, 'let me count the ways'?"

I blink at him in disbelief. "You're quoting Elizabeth Barrett Browning to me?"

He shrugs. "Maybe?"

I let out a laugh. "Who are you and what have you done with my boyfriend?" As the word leaves my mouth, we both stop moving, the atmosphere around us suddenly shifting.

"What did you say?" he asks, his gaze burning into mine.

"I meant to say, who are you and what have you done with the guy ... I'm ... err, seeing at the moment."

Don't let anyone tell you I'm not super smooth.

"Not that."

I swallow down a lump that's forming in my throat. "Not seeing?" I ask weakly.

"The boyfriend part. I like hearing that." Not that I thought it possible, but the intensity in his eyes ramps up a notch, and my pulse thuds like a giant's footsteps.

"I guess then ... that would make me your girlfriend," I say, my voice trembling.

"My girlfriend," he repeats, a smile teasing his deeply, deeply kissable lips. "Yeah. I like the sound of that. For now, anyway."

Oh, my. Is he really insinuating what I think he's insinuating? Because that would be beyond all things amazing. In a burst of euphoria, I loop my hands behind his neck, get up on my tippy toes, and press my lips against his, not caring we're in the middle of a party, surrounded by people.

He responds by pulling me closer, his big hands spanning across my back, his kiss full of want for me, need for me. Love for me.

"Sealed with a kiss, girlfriend," he murmurs.

"Break it up, you two. This is a family show," a deep voice says, and I blink at Dan's teammate, Dawson, who slaps Dan on the back, a broad grin on his face.

"Can't a guy celebrate a big win with his girl?" Dan replies, and I swear, my heart doubles in size.

His girl.

"Your girl, huh?" Emmy asks, appearing at Dawson's side. "Is there something you need to tell me, brother?"

"Like it isn't obvious," Dawson says on a laugh. "The guy blows a kiss to her from the ice every time he so much as makes contact with the puck."

Emmy points between us. "He's right. If you're trying to fly under the radar, you failed. Big time."

"You look like a big heart-shaped blob on a radar," Dawson says.

"A heart-shaped blob?" Dan asks, shaking his head. "Where do you come up with these things?"

Dawson shrugs. "I've got a reference book with great one-liners."

Both Dan and I turn to Emmy.

"Why are you looking at me?" she asks.

"You're the one with the bookstore," I reply.

Emmy laughs. "I would never sell a book with one-liners describing a couple as a heart-shaped blob on a radar."

"You should definitely stock a book like that. They would fly off the shelves," Dan tells her.

"I'll look into it," Emmy replies, clearly not intending to ever get a book with one-liners that describe people as heart-shaped blobs. "Right now, I need the ladies.' Wanna come with me, Keira?" she asks, but she doesn't wait for a reply, instead taking me by the hand and leading me across the room.

I glance back at Dan. He is watching us with a goofy grin on his handsome face, and I feel a surge of happiness fill my blood stream.

Dan and I official. We are girlfriend and boyfriend once more.

Talk about life turning out in the most unexpected—and most hoped for—way.

Once safely inside the ladies,' Emmy leans against the basin, her arms crossed. "You and my brother, huh? Talk about déjà vu. This is giving me total high school vibes."

I couldn't wipe the smile from my face if I wanted to.

"I guess it does."

Her face breaks into a smile. "I cannot tell you how happy I am. I mean, everyone knows you guys have been seeing each other, but I didn't know how serious you were."

"I guess I've never forgotten him, and it turns out, he's never forgotten me, either."

"I know he's my brother, so it's kind of weird to think of him being in a romantic relationship and all that, but the fact it's with you. Well, that makes me so happy."

"It makes me happy, too," I reply, and she pulls me in for a hug.

"I've had a lot of soda, so I need to use the facilities," she says as she gestures toward the stalls.

"Go right ahead." I turn to look in the mirror and push my hair back from my face. Knowing I was going to be looked at when Dan inevitably blew me a kiss at the game tonight, Clara helped me apply some makeup. I've got mascara, eyeliner, and even managed some lip gloss—although that was well and truly kissed off by a certain Ice Breakers captain only moments ago.

"Who knows? You might be joining the family before too long," Emmy calls out from one of the stalls.

I try not to let my heart leap at the thought, but she's the second person to suggest such a thing in the last few minutes—the first being the man himself. So that's exactly what my heart does: leap past the clouds, as high as Mount Rainier.

There's some chatter outside the ladies' before a girl explodes into the bathroom, followed by another in quick succession, filling the space with their laughter. I recognize them as a couple of the gorgeous women who've been attending each of the Ice Breakers games, wearing their cute outfits, complete with bunny ears tonight. Seriously, they look more like they belong in a Hugh Hefner nightclub than at a hockey after game party.

"Oh, it's you," says one of them, her smile dropping as her eyes land on me.

I've seen her around a bunch of times. From the Maple Fest, where she flirted with Dan at the signing table, to both the Ice Breakers games. She was one of the women who cornered Dan after the first game.

Mom always taught us that it's better to make a friend rather than an enemy, so I smile at her and say, "Hi, I'm Keira."

"Oh, I know who you are. We all do," she replies, and her friend nods in agreement, her eyes sweeping over me—and finding me wanting. "You're the girl who's somehow managed to pin Dan Roberts down."

"Well, I'd hardly say I've pinned him down—" I begin to protest.

"Oh, you have, honey. Although how?" She sweeps her eyes over me once more. "I'm not so sure. Maybe Dan likes the mannish type?"

Her friend sniggers.

I press my lips together. I had to deal with catty comments from girls before when I was with Dan in high school. Mom always said they were only jealous, so I shouldn't let them bother me. After all, she reasoned I had Dan and they didn't.

The woman who looks like a walking Instagram filter leans on the counter beside me, peering in the mirror as she dabs on some more makeup to her already flawlessly made-up face. "The way I see it, Dan's remembering what it was like to date you back in the day. He'll have his little walk down memory lane and then come to his senses." She turns to look at me. "A girl like you can't hold on to a man like Dan Roberts for long."

I open my mouth to respond, not even sure what I'm going to say. *I've just become his girlfriend? He loves me? He's never forgotten me?*

All of it sounds ridiculous—because you know what? She's probably right. Sure, Dan has feelings for me, but is it only because he's back here in our hometown, remembering what it was like to be with me back in the day?

Is what we have actually real?

Will he leave me after the last game is played?

Am I enough for Dan Roberts, NHL star?

I can't stop doubts bouncing around my mind like kids in a bouncy house.

"Come on. You can't be that naïve. Hockey players aren't exactly known as one-woman guys. Well, maybe one woman a night." She smirks at me as though she's made a funny joke, when inside, my hopes are dropping like a lead balloon.

"Dan's not like that," I protest, lifting my chin in defiance.

She gives me a knowing look. "Really? How do you know?"

I trust Dan, just as I did back in high school. He never said or did anything to make me feel otherwise. But it feels different now. Back then it was just the girls in our class. He made it clear to them that we were together, and he wasn't interested.

I open my mouth to respond, but no words come out.

She gives me a self-satisfied smirk. "You know I'm right."

The door to the ladies' swings open, and Blair appears. She takes one look at my face, darts her gaze to the women, and asks, "Are these girls bothering you, Kiki?"

"They're … uhh …," I begin, but words seem to have deserted me.

She glares at the women.

"What's with you?" asks the one who made me feel the size of a mouse.

Blair crosses her arms across her chest. "I could ask the exact same thing."

Emmy appears at the door of one of the stalls. "They were being nasty to Kiki," she says.

"I think you'll find we were just pointing out some home truths to your girl here, so you can all just back off," she replies.

"Why don't you back off all the way out of this party?" Blair suggests. Well, it's less of a suggestion and more of a threat from where I'm standing—and I could kiss her for it.

The woman bristles. "Oh, yeah? Who died and made you queen?"

Blair leans in closer to her, and says in a quiet and decidedly threatening tone, "I work in PR, and I know people. Influential people. People who could make or break anyone they want. So, I suggest you do as I say and leave this party before I feel inclined to call one of my friends."

The girls share an uncertain look before Ms. Instagram Filter raises her chin in defiance. "You're gonna make me?"

Blair nods. "I am."

The girls share another look.

"Lana, let's just go. It's a dumb party, anyway," the brunette says.

Lana throws me a final glare before both women turn on their heels and leave.

"Remind me never to cross *you*," Emmy says as she gives Blair a high five. "You were excellent!"

"All in a day's work," Blair replies with a smile. "You okay, Kiki?"

"Yeah, thanks," I reply, although after what that woman just said to me, I'm very far from okay.

"You know I've always got your back," Blair says.

"I do, too. Especially when it comes to women like that. Women who make themselves feel better by putting other women down," Emmy says.

"Long live the sisterhood. Am I right?" Blair asks, and we all agree with her.

But Lana's words have cut deep. I can't hold onto a man like Dan. I can't compete in his world, a world I know nothing about, a world so far removed from my life here in Maple Falls it may as well be on another planet.

As we return to the party, I know my mind is made-up. When the dust settles after the last game, when the team is gone, I'll have my memories of how Dan and I shone bright one last time before he left town, destined once more for bigger and brighter things.

CHAPTER 15
DAN

THE CLOCK READS thirty seconds left in the third period. It's a tie game against the Lumberjacks, 2-2. I don't want a tie in the final Ice Breakers' game. I want a win—and I know my teammates are just as hungry for it as I am.

The atmosphere in the arena is nothing short of electric. The crowd wants the win, just as much as we do.

My legs burn as I race toward the puck, but there's no time to think about that now, not with a win within our grasp, and the time on the clock ticking.

We need one final push for a goal. With literally seconds to go in the final period, Scotty's voice cuts through the noise, shouting for a pass. Due to unforeseen circumstances within the team, he's gone from coach to player for this, our final game, and right now, he's definitely proving his worth.

I glance over, my breath heavy, my lungs on fire. And there Scotty is, exactly where I want him to be to make the shot. I slap the puck his way, feeling the connection through my stick. Scotty catches it cleanly, like the expert player he was back in the day, weaving easily through the opposing defense, like a thread through a needle. It's poetry in motion watching him glide, and I wonder if this game will be the clincher in deciding whether to go back to the game as a player.

I dig my skates in as I chase after him, searching for any opening I can. Scotty's eyes meet mine for a split second, communicating exactly what he needs me to know, before he flicks the puck back at me, passing me the assist.

He sees as clearly as I do that the net is in my sights. I can make it. I can *do this*.

With every ounce of strength left in my tired body, I line up my shot and give an almighty swing at the puck. I hold my breath as it sails through the air, as though in slow motion, past the Jack's goalie's glove. It crashes into the back of the net just before the red light blares.

We did it. *We did it!*

The crowd erupts in elated cries and chants for the Ice Breakers, for me, for all of us.

We won, and I got the winning goal—with an expert assist from Scotty.

There really is nothing like it, this feeling you get when you're up against it, victory in your sights, and you risk it all for the win.

My teammates pile on me, shouting and laughing. They're all so heavy, I can barely stay on my feet. It's hard to stand when a pack of big burly guys hurls themselves at you.

Scotty pulls me into a tight hug, both of us breathless and grinning.

"Great pass," I say, my voice hoarse from shouting.

"Great shot," he returns, clapping me on the back.

Elated, I turn from him to find Keira in the crowd. She's on her feet, along with her friends and family and the rest of the town, grinning and waving and jumping up and down in glee. I skate over to the plexiglass in front of her, just as I have after every goal and at the end of each match, thumping my chest with my gloved hand before I blow her a kiss.

Just as she has every time before, she has a mixture of pride, happiness, and embarrassment on her pretty face.

That's my girl. My Kiki.

It doesn't get much better than this, people. Making the final shot to win the last game, closing out the series, and all of it in front of the woman I love.

Today has got to be as close to perfect as a day can get.

We line up to pay our respects to the Jacks before we all take a well-earned victory lap of the rink to the team song. "Ice Ice Baby" may not be a song I ever particularly liked before, but today, I'm a total convert, so much so, I'd say it's now my favorite song.

The crowd goes wild, a ripple of cheering and squeals of delight following us as we move slowly around the ice as a team. I've led these fine players over the last five games, and it has been both an honor and deeply satisfying to do so on my home turf for a worthy cause, in front of my family, my friends from before I left for the NHL, and in front of Keira.

By the time we've done our third victory lap, I gesture to the guys that it's time to bid our final farewell, and we wave at the crowd one final time as we leave the ice.

The atmosphere in the locker room is electric, everyone pumped that we not only won the final game, but that we won the series, too. With it is a tinge of sadness, too. It's been great to work with these guys—even Cooper Montgomery with his perpetual scowl. He's a good guy and a great player. Playing with Dawson again after all this time brought back great memories of our college years together, and it's with tears in my eyes that I slap him on the back as we hug.

"Awesome defense today," I say. "I'm gonna miss having you on my team."

"It's been real, man," he replies. "Let's try to spend more time together in the future, when our schedules allow."

I grin, knowing I've rekindled an important friendship in my life. "You got it."

As the captain, of course, there's the press conference that follows, and this time it's an absolute pleasure to front for the team, sharing my genuine pride in our success on the ice.

"Where are you going next now that you're over your injury? Back to the Blizzard?" a journalist asks.

"I'm headed back to Chicago for my day job tomorrow morning, but I do plan on spending a lot more time Maple Falls in the future. This place is home to me, and being back here has reminded me of that," I reply, searching the crowd for Keira. I don't find her, which is weird. She usually comes to these postgame press conferences. In fact, she's never missed one, always at the back of the room, her presence reassuring me.

"Any particular reason for that?" the journalist asks, refocussing my attention.

"It's my hometown and I've missed it here. My family. My friends." I spot Mom, Dad, Emmy, and Mimi in the crowd. Each and every one of them is smiling proudly back at me, and it warms me to know I was able to lead the team to a victory here in my hometown arena in front of them. Although they've all seen me playing for the Blizzard in recent years, it means so much more when it's on home turf—and for such a meaningful cause.

"Does that have anything to do with the person you've been blowing kisses to over the last five games here?"

I can't help but smile at the thought of Keira. "Maybe," I

reply elusively, but anyone who knows me could read my expression from a hundred yards away.

The press conference finally wraps, and I shake Zach Hart's hand.

"Thanks for all your hard work, Dan," he says.

"It's been an honor and a pleasure, sir," I say.

"You've been a great leader for the team, just as Troy said you would be. And enough with the 'sir.' It's Zach."

"Zach. You got it."

"You can call me sir, if you like," Troy says, resting an arm on his brother's shoulder.

I laugh. "Never gonna happen, man," I tell him with a grin. I give him a hug. "Thanks for including me in this. It's been … life changing."

His brows pop up toward his hairline. "Life changing? High praise indeed."

I grin at him, confident in the decision I've made, a decision that will see me back in Maple Falls more often, and, one day permanently. It's an idea that began forming in my mind over the last few weeks as I've spent more and more time with Keira. It's an idea that feels so right, I wonder why I never thought of it before. I guess I was so busy building my hockey career, always driving forward to be the best player I could be, to be captain of the team, to make a name for myself, that I forgot to stop and be with the people who matter the most. To be in the place that matters the most.

"I'll see you 'round a bit more. I plan on spending more time here as my schedule allows it," I say.

"Your wrist is okay now?"

"Like new."

"In that case, you'll be needing to get back to the Blizzard, but I hope you do come back here more often. It's been good having you around, and the fans? They sure do love you."

"What can I say? I'm the Maple Falls hometown hero." I throw him a wink as we laugh together, because as much as it feels good to have the love of the crowd, there really is only one person whose love matters to me the most.

As I make my way to my car, I pull out my phone and message Keira.

> ME:
>
> Everything okay? I didn't see you at the press conference. I'm heading to the wrap party now. xoxo

I hit send and wait for a reply. The three little dots appear on my phone, telling me she's responding. Then they disappear.

Weird.

I climb into my car and send her another message.

> ME:
>
> Are you already at the party?

This time there aren't even any little dots, telling me she's tapping out a reply. I figure she's probably busy talking to somebody at the party, and I take the short drive to the Rustic Slice Pizzeria, which has been booked out for us tonight.

Pushing through the door, I'm hit by the warmth of the restaurant, the delicious smell of pizza filling my nose, laughter and chatter in the air. I search the place for Keira, but don't spot her. Instead, I find Mom and Dad, who wave me over.

I greet them both with warm hugs.

"We are so proud of you—do you know that?" Mom says as she reaches up to smooth out my hair. Such a motherly thing to do.

"I do know," I say kindly. "I owe you a lot. Both of you."

"We'd do it all again, son," Dad says, clasping my shoulder. "All of it."

"Thanks," I say, choked up. "It's like I invented a cure for cancer or something."

"Winning a hockey season comes a close second," Dad jokes.

"Mimi wanted to be here for the after-party, but she was a

little tired after the game, so we took her home, but she said to give you this." Mom places a kiss against my cheek.

"Thanks. Hey, have you seen Keira around? I figured she was here," I say.

"If she's not already, I'm sure she'll be here soon. Half the town's here tonight to celebrate, and we know she's your special someone." Mom's eyes sparkle as her face creases in a knowing smile. "I always liked that one, you know."

I beam back at her, my heart full. "Yeah. Me, too."

"Pizza slice?" a waitress asks, thrusting a large tray in front of me. "Oh, it's you. Great work tonight, Dan."

"Thanks. It was a team effort," I reply as I take a slice.

"Sure, but they couldn't have done it without Dan the Man," she replies.

"You got that right," Dad agrees, still beaming proudly.

All this adoration could go to a guy's head. Maybe it's a good thing I'm heading back to Chicago in the morning, even if I don't want to leave.

"Thanks for this," I tell the waitress as I take a bite of pizza. "I'm going to go find Keira," I say to my family. "Catch you later?"

"Sure thing," my sister says as Mom says, "Anything for the hero of the hour."

Seriously, too much adulation can't be good for a guy.

I circle the room, stopping to talk to teammates and old school friends, looking for Keira. With no sign, I pull my phone out once more to check for messages. What I read makes me stop in my tracks.

> KEIRA:
> Dan. The past few weeks have meant so much to me, and I know I will never forget you.

Something unpleasant squirms inside. What is she saying? She'll never forget me?

There's another message.

THE REBOUND PLAY

> **KEIRA:**
> It's completely spineless to do this by text, but I know if I see you I'll cave. You're leaving tomorrow morning, and I think it's for the best that we say our goodbyes.

What the …? She cannot be serious. After everything … she's breaking up with me?

There's one final message.

> **KEIRA:**
> I'm sorry, Dan. I will always love you.

I blink at the screen, barely believing the words. Tension tightens my chest, a knot twisting painfully in my belly.

Keira doesn't want to be with me? She loves me but it's *over*?

No. I can't believe it. I *won't* believe it. Whatever is going on with her right now, wherever her head is, I need to see her. Reason with her. Show her that I love her and want to be with her, no matter what.

I won't let her end this. We are meant to be together. I've always known it, but I've never fully allowed myself to embrace it. Now that I have, there's no way on this sweet earth I'm going to let her go.

With my mind made-up, I charge to the exit, determined. As I make my way through the crowd of people, I feel a hand on my forearm and look up to see Cooper's PR person, Blair.

"I know where she is," she says without preamble, and I snap my attention to her. She doesn't need to mention Keira's name.

I lock my jaw, my body taut with tension, determined to find her and make this right. "Tell me where."

CHAPTER 16
KEIRA

"NEXT TO BEING MARRIED, a girl likes to be crossed a little in love now and then."

I close my dog-eared copy of *Pride and Prejudice* over in disgust. Are you serious, Mr. Bennet? No girl likes to be crossed a little in love. *Ever*. Heartache is the worst feeling in the world. Yet still, here I am, curled up on the sofa, having crossed Dan in love only thirty-seven minutes ago.

I let out a heavy sigh, my eyes filling with tears. I did what I had to do. Although I love Dan, I know that as soon as he's back in his world, I'll end up with a broken heart when he realizes that being with me these past weeks has been nothing more than a pleasant walk down memory lane, back to a girl he once loved before he was even a man.

I don't belong in his world. It's foreign to me, and as much as I hated hearing it from Lana that night in the ladies', I knew she was speaking the truth the moment the words fell from her lips. I don't fit into his world. I'm not the kind of woman someone like Dan Roberts will end up with. I'm a small-town girl whose life revolves around her family and her town. I'm not glamorous. I'm not worldly.

I'm not enough.

"Are you okay?" Clara asks as she pads into the living room in her thick socks, her robe wrapped tightly around her slim waist.

"No," I choke out, my voice strangled by emotion.

She sits down on the sofa next to me and pulls me into a hug. "You did what you thought was right, honey."

"Then why does it hurt so much?" I sob into her shoulder.

"Because you love him. It's as simple as that."

I sniff and brush the tears from my eyes. "If only it were that simple then I would still be with him."

She presses her lips together, her eyes searching my face. "Explain to me once more why you broke up with him?"

"Clara," I warn, not wanting to go down that path again. It was painful enough the first time she asked when she found me clasping onto my knees, sobbing like a child.

She raises her hands in the air. "All I'm saying is you love him and it's pretty dang obvious that he loves you, too."

My stupid, stupid heart leaps at the thought that Dan loves me.

"But it's not that easy," I protest. "It's ... complicated."

"What love isn't complicated?"

"The easy kind, like Mom and Dad had."

"Do you wanna know what I think?" she asks, but in typical older sister style, she doesn't wait for my response. "I think love is a hot mess. It's complicated, sure, but it is *so* worth it."

I shake my head, my throat hot. "It won't be worth it. Not for me. It will end in tears, and I'll be left alone, right here where I always am."

"You don't know that."

"I do."

She studies me for a beat before she lets out a sigh. "Well, I guess you've made your mind up."

"I have."

"Can I say one more thing?"

I sniff. "Can I stop you?"

"The heart wants what the heart wants, even when it makes no sense."

Fresh tears spring to my eyes. "Not helping, sis."

She places her hand on my shoulder and gives it a squeeze. "You've got to do what's right for you. And right now, I've got to do what's right for me and that means heading to bed." She pushes herself up off the sofa.

"Sleep well."

"Hang in there."

As Clara heads to bed, I pick up my book again and accidentally reread Mr. Bennet's line about wanting to be crossed in love and close it again. What was I thinking reading a Jane Austen novel? I need to read a thriller or a grisly crime novel. Anything but a love story with a happily ever after.

I collect a few tissues from the Kleenex box on the coffee table and wipe my eyes. I'll go to see Emmy tomorrow. She'll give me some recommendations for some anti-love books.

I switch off the lamp and head to the bathroom when there's a loud knock on the door. I almost leap out of my skin in shock.

"Who's there?" I call out.

"It's me, Dan," a muffled voice replies, and my heart leaps into my mouth at the thought that he's here—even though the last thing I want right now is to have to see him. Because if I do, I know I will crumble, my resolve gone, and I will willingly fall into his arms.

"Please, Kiki. Let me in. Let's talk about this."

I stand, rooted to the spot, indecision playing racquetball with my brain.

"I don't want to lose you," he says and my heart screams at me to open that door.

I make my way down the hallway until all that lies between us is our wooden front door with its frosted pane of glass. "Please go, Dan. It's for the best. You'll see."

"Kiki, please. I love you and I don't want to lose you."

It's like the sincerity in his words has a direct line to my heart, and before I know what I'm doing, I've pulled the door open to see him standing on the welcome mat in his post-match clothes, looking more handsome than I've ever seen him in my life. There's pain etched across his face, and the deepest look of love in his eyes.

Neither of us utters a word. We simply stand on either side of the door frame for a beat, staring at one another, a world of unspoken words swirling around us.

He makes the first move, stepping closer, pulling me into his arms in one smooth, purposeful movement, and I find myself melting into his arms as he presses an urgent kiss against my lips.

"I love you. I love you," he murmurs against my mouth between kisses, his arms holding me possessively against his firm body.

I want to let go of all my fears, of everything I know to be true, and stay here in his arms, confident in his love for me.

But I can't. Not when I know that we live in different worlds and that one day, he will see that.

With the strength of Hercules himself, I pull back from him, and I'm shocked to see the tracks of his tears on his cheeks. I reach up to touch them with my fingertips. "I'm sorry. I'm sorry, so sorry."

"Don't be sorry. Be happy that we're together. Know that this is what is meant to be."

I twist my mouth. "Why don't you come inside." I take him by the hand and lead him down the hallway to the living room.

Once inside, he closes the door behind us.

I clasp my hands at my waist, more to stop myself from pulling him to me than anything else.

"Can I tell you one thing, Kiki?" he asks.

I nod, not trusting myself to speak.

"We've got this second chance, which is more than most people get in this life. The last thing I'm going to do is give up on you. Give up on *us*. I love you, with every fiber of my being. And I know you love me, too."

"But Dan,—"

"If this is what you really want, then tell me and I'll walk away forever. But I think you're letting your fears get the most of you, and I'm here to tell you that you've got nothing to fear because I love you and I will never, ever hurt you. I give you my word."

"It was so hard when you left the first time. I know we agreed to break up, but I didn't want to, and I never got over it. I can't put myself through that again."

He cradles my face in his hands and says tenderly, "You won't have to because I will never leave you."

"But ... but your team. Chicago. The NHL."

"My mind's made up. I'm giving it a year, during which you can visit me as often as you want, and I can come home here to see you whenever I can. And then, once I'm done with the Blizzard at the end of next season, I'll move back here to be with you."

As he reaches for me, my fears begin to evaporate around me.

My eyes widen to the size of hockey pucks. "You're going to move back to Maple Falls?" I ask, my voice a mere whisper.

A smile pulls at the edges of his mouth, lighting up his whole face. "It's home. *You're* home. I let you go once before, Kiki. I'll never make that mistake again."

And with that, he pulls me against him, wrapping his arms around me, and kisses me with such love, it brings tears of joy to my eyes.

"I love you," I murmur.

"You know what else?" he asks.

A bubble of giddy laughter rises up inside of me. "There's more?"

"One day—and I'm not going to tell you when—I'm going to ask you to be my wife."

"And I will say yes," I whisper into his ear, the last vestige of fear flying away on the wings of his commitment, my heart soaring along with it.

"I love you, my Kiki."

CHAPTER 17
DAN

THE CLOCK TICKS down in the final period, and we're down 3-1 against the Jacks, the team I want to beat so bad, I can taste it. I can sense the tension in the air, and every member of the Blizzard is pushing their limits. As their captain, it's my job to lead by example, and that's what I do as I see an opening, deep in the final period.

Puck on my stick, I skate down the ice, dodging defenders like they're standing still. Out of the corner of my eye, I spot Nick, our new rookie recruit, fresh from college, in the perfect position near the net. He's ready, eager, and instinctively, I know this is his moment.

With a quick flick of my wrist, I send the puck his way. It's a perfect pass, sliding through the chaos of skates and sticks. Just as I'd planned, Nick pulls back his stick and fires a shot.

As I watch, time seems to slow. The puck sails past the Jacks' goalie, hitting the back of the net with a satisfying *thud*. The arena erupts in ecstatic cheers as I skate over to Nick and collect his bulky frame in a hug. Nick's face is a mix of disbelief and pure joy.

"Great job, kid," I say, proud of him and our team.

"Plenty more where that came from," he replies with a grin.

We scramble for the next play, taking our chances where we can. At 3-2 down, we've got nothing to lose, but as the final horn blares, we've lost. Despite it, I'm proud of my team, and I'm proud of myself. What a way to end my career as captain of the Chicago Blizzard, a position I've held since returning to Chicago from Maple Falls.

I spot Keira in the stands, standing with Emmy, my parents, and Mimi, who made the journey to Chicago for my final NHL match, despite her health. Alongside my family is Clara with her kids, Benny—who made it onto a team this year and is now officially a hockey addict—and Hannah, still a figure-skating princess. Clara being here is a big deal. She's not left Maple Falls since she was diagnosed with CFS. But lately, she is managing her health enough that she's been able to spend more time with her kids, and even hold down a part-time job, doing admin for a business in downtown Maple Falls.

As I always have since those games back in Maple Falls, I skate over to the plexiglass and blow Keira a kiss, and as usual, people swivel to see, and applause radiates through the arena.

It turns out, people love a second-chance love story—and I'm more than happy to have provided them with ours.

It's become our thing, my blowing Keira a kiss at the end of each game, win or lose. People talk about it in the media and love to speculate over how long we'll last and when I'm going to put a ring on it.

They'll get their answer to both of those questions soon enough.

After a team debrief in the locker room, Coach leads a standing ovation for me, thanking me for my service to the team as both a player and, in the last year, as the team captain. There's a party for me to say goodbye to everyone tomorrow night, and it's with an odd sense of pride, nostalgia, and a touch of regret that I say goodbye to both the team and the arena, the place where so many of my memories have been made.

But tonight isn't about the past. It's about the future. My future, to be specific.

I pull my car into my driveway and take a moment before I head inside. I know Keira is in there with her sister and niece and nephew, along with my whole family, Ethan included. They've all been such important parts of my life, each of them, and as I sit in the dark, I say a little prayer of gratitude for them all.

It takes many to make the career of one, and I've been so very lucky to have this group of people by my side, every step of the way.

The house is filled with soft music and chatter as I enter it and look around. With its high ceilings and wide staircase, hardwood floors and expensive art, all it is to me is a house. Soon, I'll be moving back to Maple Falls where I intend to make a home.

I step into the living room, and everyone greets me with hugs and kisses and congratulations. Mom is busy making sure everyone is fed with Emmy as her helper; my brother, Ethan, visiting from some movie set in Europe, is topping off people's drinks; Dad is telling stories of my youth and expressing how proud he is of his son's hockey career; Clara is listening dutifully as her kids yawn. It's way past their bedtime, but everyone knew they wouldn't want to miss my last NHL game, least of all Benny.

And then there's Keira. She's talking to my mom and Emmy, smiling warmly, wearing my jersey, and looking so unbelievably beautiful, it makes me catch my breath. She turns to me and smiles, and I stride over to her to pull her into a kiss.

"How was it?" she asks.

"It was ... well, it was a lot of things."

"I bet it was. Did Coach get all misty eyed as he said goodbye to you?"

I think of Coach O'Donnell, this big, former player, and how he choked back tears as he gave his speech in the locker room. "A little."

"They're so going to miss you."

I press another kiss to her lips. "They'll just have to come visit us."

Her face creases into her beautiful smile.

Suddenly, it's urgent I do what I plan on doing tonight. "Wait right here, okay? I'll be right back," I say.

"I wouldn't want to be anywhere else."

I give Ethan a gesture, and he follows me into the dining room.

"Have you got it?" I ask.

"Of course I do." He flashes me his Hollywood smile. "You ready for this?"

A sense of peace envelops me. Peace, joy, and love.

"Sure am," I say.

"Well then, let's do this."

I collect a glass and spoon from the sideboard and, holding them up, I clink them together to get everyone's attention. As all eyes land on me, I hold my hand out for Keira, who slips past Emmy to be by my side.

"Speech time, huh?" she says.

"Something like that," I murmur to her before I address the

room. "As you all know, tonight was my final game for the Blizzard. Being a part of the team, and in the last year, being their captain, has been a dream come true for me, a dream I know many of you have had active involvement in over the years. Mom, Dad, I'm looking at you."

"We love you, honey," Mom says.

"Tonight marks the end of one chapter, and it's also the beginning of another one, one that's bringing me home to Maple Falls. But there's one small thing I need to take care of before I get on that plane with you all in a couple days."

"Sell the house?" Dad asks, and people laugh.

I smile. "There's that, too, but this is a slightly more personal thing."

Ethan pulls a small blue box from his pocket and hands it to me. Several people suck in a breath, knowing what's coming next, and as I turn to Keira and take both her hands in mine, she smiles up at me, softening me to Jell-O.

"Dan? Wh-what are you doing?" she asks, a tremble in her voice.

"Keira. Kiki. You were my first love, and my last, and I cannot imagine my life without you in it." I lower myself onto one knee, open the ring box, her hand held in mine. "Will you do me the very great honor of marrying me?"

Her hand flies to her chest, her face lifting into the dimpled smile I so adore. "Oh, Dan, yes. Yes! I'll marry you."

I slide the ring onto her finger. A perfect fit. I share a smile with Clara, who waggles her brows at me. It was Clara who told me what size ring to get, and I swore her to secrecy, which, judging by the way Keira's hand is trembling right now, she stuck to.

"Dan, it's so beautiful," she says, gazing down into the diamond. She lifts her face to mine, tears tumbling down her cheeks. "Thank you."

"You're the one that's beautiful," I say softly. "I love you, the future Keira Roberts." I pull her close to me and brush a soft and tender kiss against her lips as everyone cheers and applauds.

When I'd decided that tonight was the night I was going to ask Keira to be my wife, Ethan had suggested I do it on the ice at tonight's game, in front of the world. But that's not Keira's style. She's more of a family person, never seeking the limelight, and I know everyone in this room means so much to her. I wanted them to share in our happiness, too.

Everyone congratulates us, pulling us into earnest, loving hugs, raising their glasses to toast us, and it's impossible not to feel the love that fills the room to bursting.

In a few days we'll all be back in Maple Falls. I'll be readying myself to teach kids how to play hockey at Troy and Kelly's arena and taking my position as coach of the high school team, too. Keira will be back at the Maple Falls Farmers' Market in the town she loves, and our new lives will begin. And I know I'll be right back where I belong, with my first love, my only love, my Kiki.

Do you want to know what happens next? For a BONUS EPILOGUE set in Dan and Keira's future, follow this link: https://BookHip.com/VLARSHM

. . .

Do you want to read more about Dan's team, the Chicago Blizzard? Meet the rest of the team in Kate's romcom, get *Mistletoe Face Off* here: https://books2read.com/MistletoeFaceOff

KEIRA'S GLUTEN-FREE PUMPKIN PIE RECIPE

Ingredients

1 x 9-inch store-bought gluten-free pie crust, deep dish, unbaked

3/4 cup granulated sugar

1/2 teaspoon salt

2 teaspoon ground cinnamon

3/4 teaspoon ground ginger

1/2 teaspoon ground cloves

2 large free range eggs

15 ounce fresh pumpkin puree (roast 2-inch cubes of pumpkin for 30 mins at 375 degrees F)

12 ounce can evaporated milk

Instructions

1. Preheat oven to 425 degrees F.
2. In a large bowl beat the eggs and pumpkin puree together.
3. In a separate bowl combine the sugar, cinnamon, salt, ginger, and cloves
4. Add the dry ingredients to the wet pumpkin mixture.
5. Gradually stir in the evaporated milk.

6. Carefully pour mixture into the unbaked pie shell.

7. Bake at 425 degrees F for 15 minutes, then reduce the temperature to 350° F and bake for 45 minutes longer, or until the pie is set. You can check for doneness by placing a sharp knife inserted into the center. If it comes out clean, it's done.

9. Cool completely on a wire cooling rack. Serve immediately with whipped cream or vanilla ice cream. Enjoy!

NEXT BOOK IN THE LOVE ON THIN ICE SERIES

GRAB the next book in the series where Dawson and Emmy get their chance at love in Grace Worthington's *The Friend Face Off*. You can find it on Amazon.

Getting involved with your brother's best friend is risky enough. But when he's a hockey player? It's a whole new level of bad idea.

. . .

Emmy

As a ravenous reader, I've got a secret: I'm obsessed with hockey romances. But let me tell you, real life hockey players are nothing like my book boyfriends.

So I threw down the gauntlet on BookTok. I challenged any single guy out there to prove me wrong. Can a real hockey player be as romantic as the ones in my favorite stories?

Enter Dawson Hayes, a goalie with a point to prove and my brother's best friend. He's confident he can win me over and take me on the most romantic date of my life.

But there's a catch: for me to accept, I have to pretend that he's my fake boyfriend. Now everyone in my small town thinks that Dawson and I are having a fall fling. Even if it's a fling that can't last.

Worst of all, I'm starting to believe this fling is real. I'm falling for my brother's best friend.

Dawson

The first time I met Emmy, her brother warned me to stay away. As hockey teammates, that made her totally off-limits. But now I'm back in Emmy's small town to play in a charity hockey match, and I can't resist her dating challenge: to find out if any man can be more romantic than the book boyfriends she adores.

Emmy and I are both fiercely competitive, and I'm determined to win her over.

When the moment of truth comes, the chemistry between us turns into something neither of us expected: A romantic face-off between friends who are insanely attracted to each other.

Now, I'm out to prove to her that you should never judge a book by its cover—or a hockey player when it comes to love.

You can get *The Friend Face Off* on Amazon.

CAST OF CHARACTERS IN THE LOVE ON THIN ICE SERIES

ANGEL DAVIS: love interest is Scotty MacFarland; cousins with Harlow Lemieux; collaborates with Emmy Roberts to have books at Happy Horizons Ranch.

Blair Radcliffe: love interest is Cooper Montgomery; best college friends with Keira Johnson; knows Willa Blackwell through work connections.

Cooper Montgomery: love interest is Blair Radcliffe; plays for the Tennessee Wolves; went to college with Ted "The Bear" Powell; knows Scotty MacFarland from the minor leagues; right winger, #89.

Dan Roberts: love interest is Keira Johnson; brother of Emerson (Emmy) Roberts; best college friends with Dawson Hayes; played in the Chicago Blizzard with Troy Hart; nickname is Dan the Man; center, #29.

• • •

Dawson Hayes: love interest is Emmy Roberts; college best friend of Dan Roberts; played on the Carolina Crushers; goalie, #1.

Ellie Butler: love interest is Zach Hart; friends with Keira Johnson.

Emmy Roberts: love interest is Dawson Hayes; sibling to Dan Roberts; friends with Keira Johnson.

Harlow Lemieux: love interest is Ted "The Bear" Powell; Angel Davis's cousin; friends with Willa Blackwell.

Keira Johnson: love interest is Dan Roberts; best college friends with Blair Radcliffe; friends with Angel Davis, Ellie Butler, and Emmerson Roberts.

Noah Beaumont: love interest is Willa Blackwell; former NHL superstar who now plays for the AHL team, River City Renegades; defenseman, #5.

Scotty MacFarland: love interest is Angel Davis; former player with the Denver Peaks; knows Cooper Montgomery and Ted Powell from minor league days; second coach for Ice Breakers, #14.

Ted "The Bear" Powell: love interest is Harlow Lemieux; plays for the Nebraska Knights; went to college with Cooper Montgomery; defenseman, #58.

Willa Blackwell: love interest is Noah Beaumont; college friend of Harlow Lemieux and knows Blair Radcliffe through work connections.

Zach Hart: love interest is Ellie Butler; billionaire backer of the Ice Breakers; brother of Ice Breakers' founder, Troy Hart.

ALSO IN THE LOVE ON THIN ICE SERIES

Breaking the Ice by Whitney Dineen

The Rebound Play by Kate O'Keeffe

The Friend Face Off by Grace Worthington

Love in Overtime by Melissa Baldwin

The Parent Playbook by Elsie Woods

Love on Thin Ice by Ellie Hall

Penalties and Proposals by Anne Kemp

ALSO BY KATE O'KEEFFE

HOCKEY ROMCOMS:

Mistletoe Face Off

The Rebound Play

ROYAL ROMCOMS:

The Backup Princess

Royally Matched

The Royal Runaway

SMALL TOWN ROMCOMS:

Faking It With the Grump

Faking It With My Best Friend

Faking It With the Guy Next Door

ROMCOMS SET IN BRITAIN:

Dating Mr. Darcy

Marrying Mr. Darcy

Falling for Another Darcy

Falling for Mr. Bingley (spin-off novella)

Never Fall for Your Back-Up Guy

Never Fall for Your Enemy

Never Fall for Your Fake Fiancé

Never Fall for Your One that Got Away

ROMCOMS SET IN NEW ZEALAND:

One Last First Date

Two Last First Dates

Three Last First Dates

Four Last First Dates

No More Bad Dates

No More Terrible Dates

No More Horrible Dates

Styling Wellywood

Miss Perfect Meets Her Match

Falling for Grace

CO-AUTHORED WITH MELISSA BALDWIN:

One Way Ticket

WRITING AS LACEY SINCLAIR:

Manhattan Cinderella

The Right Guy

ABOUT THE AUTHOR

Kate O'Keeffe is a *USA Today* bestselling author known for her fun, feel-good romantic comedies brimming with humor, heart, and happily ever afters. A native of New Zealand, Kate has crafted numerous popular series, garnering a devoted international readership.

With a flair for witty banter and irresistible heroines navigating the ups and downs of modern dating, Kate's novels showcase strong friendships, comedic entanglements, and the of course sometimes bumpy but always hopeful road to love.

When she's not writing, Kate can often be found reading romcoms, binging her favourite shows, or spending time with her friends and family in the beautiful Hawke's Bay region of New Zealand.

Made in United States
Troutdale, OR
04/23/2025